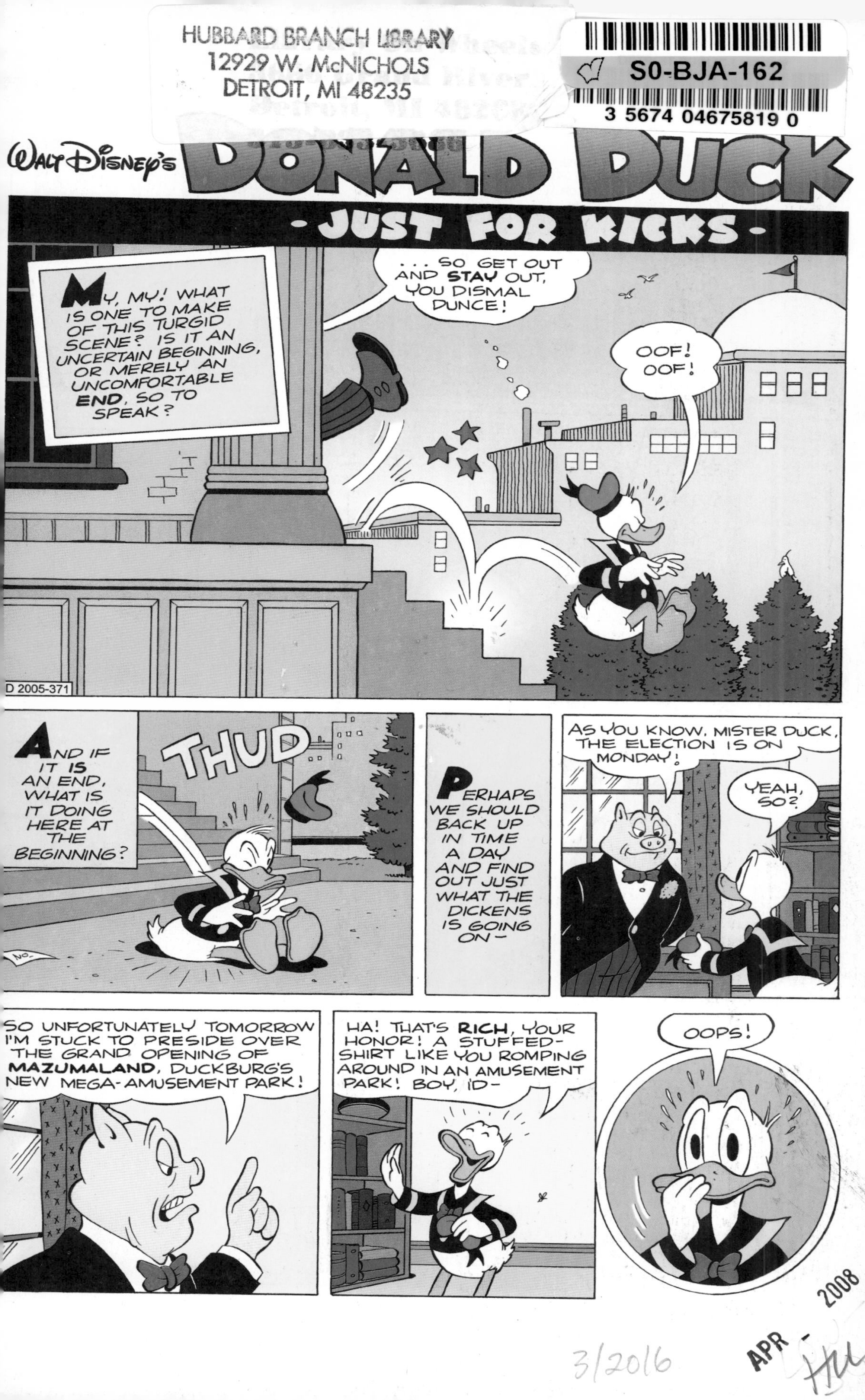
WALT DISNEY'S DONALD DUCK
·JUST FOR KICKS·
MY, MY! WHAT IS ONE TO MAKE OF THIS TURGID SCENE? IS IT AN UNCERTAIN BEGINNING, OR MERELY AN UNCOMFORTABLE END, SO TO SPEAK?
. . . SO GET OUT AND STAY OUT, YOU DISMAL DUNCE!
OOF! OOF!
D 2005-371
AND IF IT IS AN END, WHAT IS IT DOING HERE AT THE BEGINNING?
THUD
PERHAPS WE SHOULD BACK UP IN TIME A DAY AND FIND OUT JUST WHAT THE DICKENS IS GOING ON—
AS YOU KNOW, MISTER DUCK, THE ELECTION IS ON MONDAY!
YEAH, SO?
SO UNFORTUNATELY TOMORROW I'M STUCK TO PRESIDE OVER THE GRAND OPENING OF MAZUMALAND, DUCKBURG'S NEW MEGA-AMUSEMENT PARK!
HA! THAT'S RICH, YOUR HONOR! A STUFFED-SHIRT LIKE YOU ROMPING AROUND IN AN AMUSEMENT PARK! BOY, I'D—
OOPS!

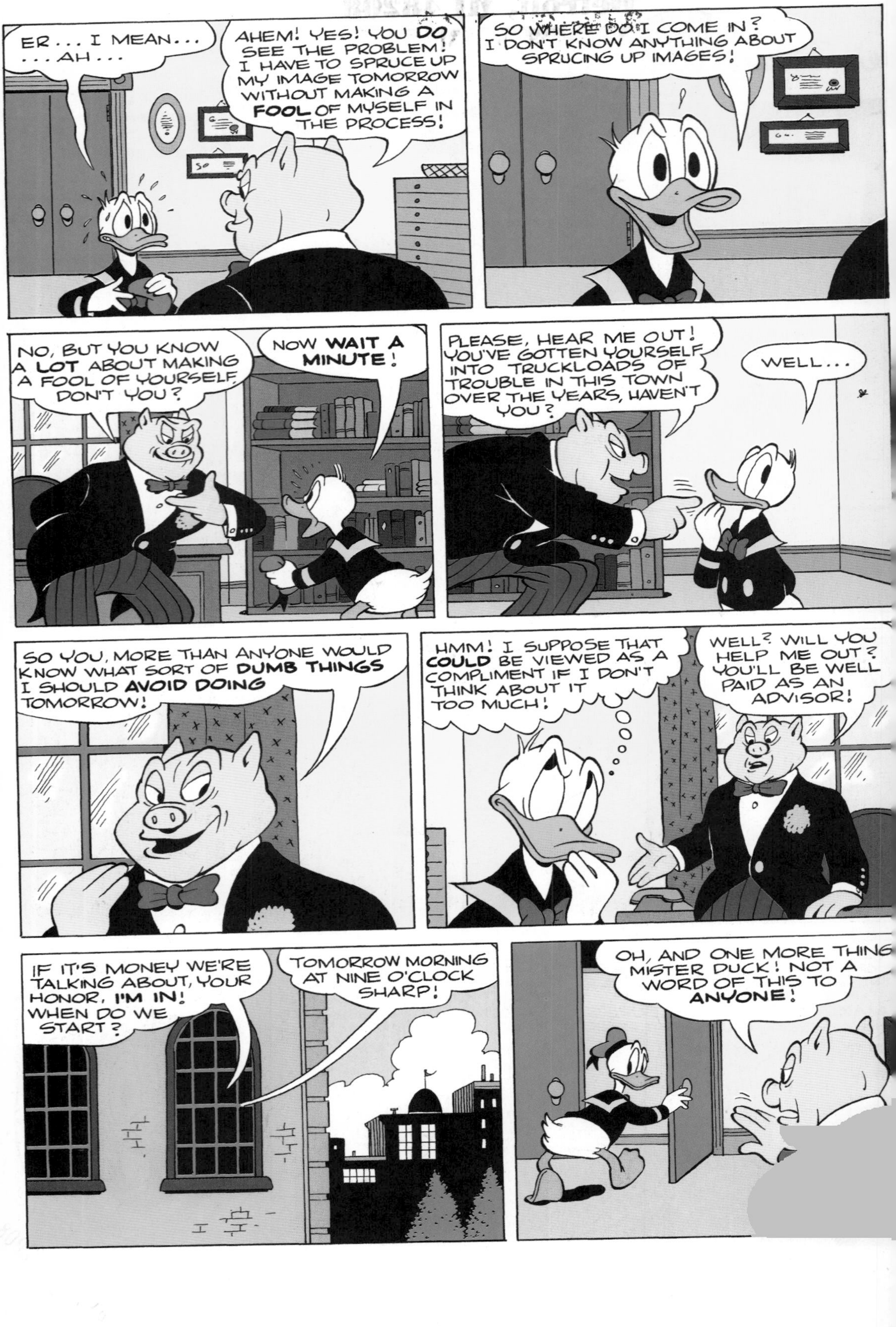
ER . . . I MEAN . . .
. . . AH . . .
AHEM! YES! YOU DO SEE THE PROBLEM! I HAVE TO SPRUCE UP MY IMAGE TOMORROW WITHOUT MAKING A FOOL OF MYSELF IN THE PROCESS!
SO WHERE DO I COME IN? I DON'T KNOW ANYTHING ABOUT SPRUCING UP IMAGES!
NO, BUT YOU KNOW A LOT ABOUT MAKING A FOOL OF YOURSELF, DON'T YOU?
NOW WAIT A MINUTE!
PLEASE, HEAR ME OUT! YOU'VE GOTTEN YOURSELF INTO TRUCKLOADS OF TROUBLE IN THIS TOWN OVER THE YEARS, HAVEN'T YOU?
WELL . . .
SO YOU, MORE THAN ANYONE WOULD KNOW WHAT SORT OF DUMB THINGS I SHOULD AVOID DOING TOMORROW!
HMM! I SUPPOSE THAT COULD BE VIEWED AS A COMPLIMENT IF I DON'T THINK ABOUT IT TOO MUCH!
WELL? WILL YOU HELP ME OUT? YOU'LL BE WELL PAID AS AN ADVISOR!
IF IT'S MONEY WE'RE TALKING ABOUT, YOUR HONOR, I'M IN! WHEN DO WE START?
TOMORROW MORNING AT NINE O'CLOCK SHARP!
OH, AND ONE MORE THING MISTER DUCK! NOT A WORD OF THIS TO ANYONE!

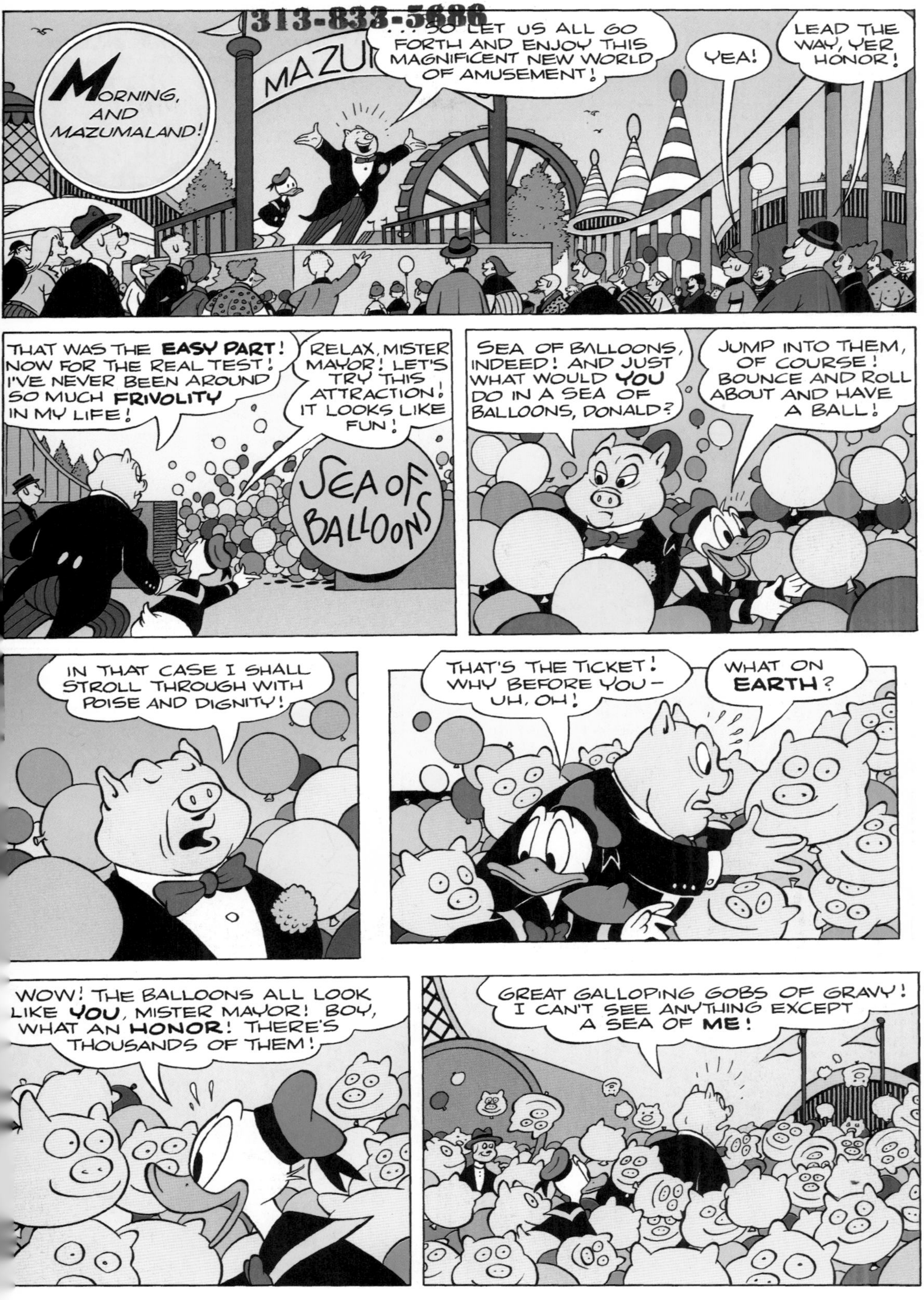
MORNING, AND MAZUMALAND!
. . . SO LET US ALL GO FORTH AND ENJOY THIS MAGNIFICENT NEW WORLD OF AMUSEMENT!
YEA!
LEAD THE WAY, YER HONOR!
THAT WAS THE EASY PART! NOW FOR THE REAL TEST! I'VE NEVER BEEN AROUND SO MUCH FRIVOLITY IN MY LIFE!
RELAX, MISTER MAYOR! LET'S TRY THIS ATTRACTION! IT LOOKS LIKE FUN!
SEA OF BALLOONS
SEA OF BALLOONS, INDEED! AND JUST WHAT WOULD YOU DO IN A SEA OF BALLOONS, DONALD?
JUMP INTO THEM, OF COURSE! BOUNCE AND ROLL ABOUT AND HAVE A BALL!
IN THAT CASE I SHALL STROLL THROUGH WITH POISE AND DIGNITY!
THAT'S THE TICKET! WHY BEFORE YOU— UH, OH!
WHAT ON EARTH?
WOW! THE BALLOONS ALL LOOK LIKE YOU, MISTER MAYOR! BOY, WHAT AN HONOR! THERE'S THOUSANDS OF THEM!
GREAT GALLOPING GOBS OF GRAVY! I CAN'T SEE ANYTHING EXCEPT A SEA OF ME!

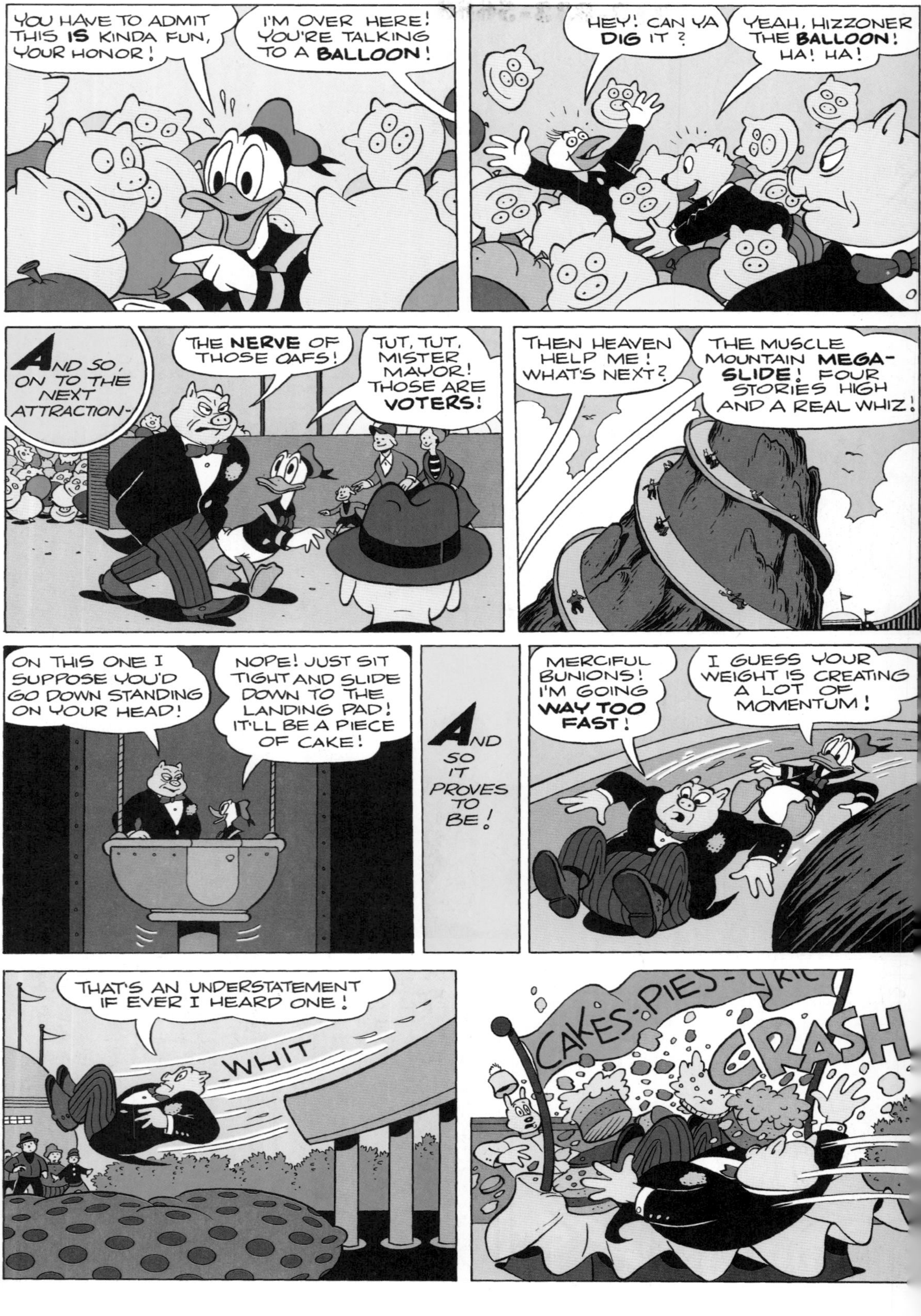
YOU HAVE TO ADMIT THIS IS KINDA FUN, YOUR HONOR!
I'M OVER HERE! YOU'RE TALKING TO A BALLOON!
HEY! CAN YA DIG IT?
YEAH, HIZZONER THE BALLOON! HA! HA!
AND SO, ON TO THE NEXT ATTRACTION-
THE NERVE OF THOSE OAFS!
TUT, TUT, MISTER MAYOR! THOSE ARE VOTERS!
THEN HEAVEN HELP ME! WHAT'S NEXT?
THE MUSCLE MOUNTAIN MEGA-SLIDE! FOUR STORIES HIGH AND A REAL WHIZ!
ON THIS ONE I SUPPOSE YOU'D GO DOWN STANDING ON YOUR HEAD!
NOPE! JUST SIT TIGHT AND SLIDE DOWN TO THE LANDING PAD! IT'LL BE A PIECE OF CAKE!
AND SO IT PROVES TO BE!
MERCIFUL BUNIONS! I'M GOING WAY TOO FAST!
I GUESS YOUR WEIGHT IS CREATING A LOT OF MOMENTUM!
THAT'S AN UNDERSTATEMENT IF EVER I HEARD ONE!
WHIT
CAKES-PIES-
CRASH

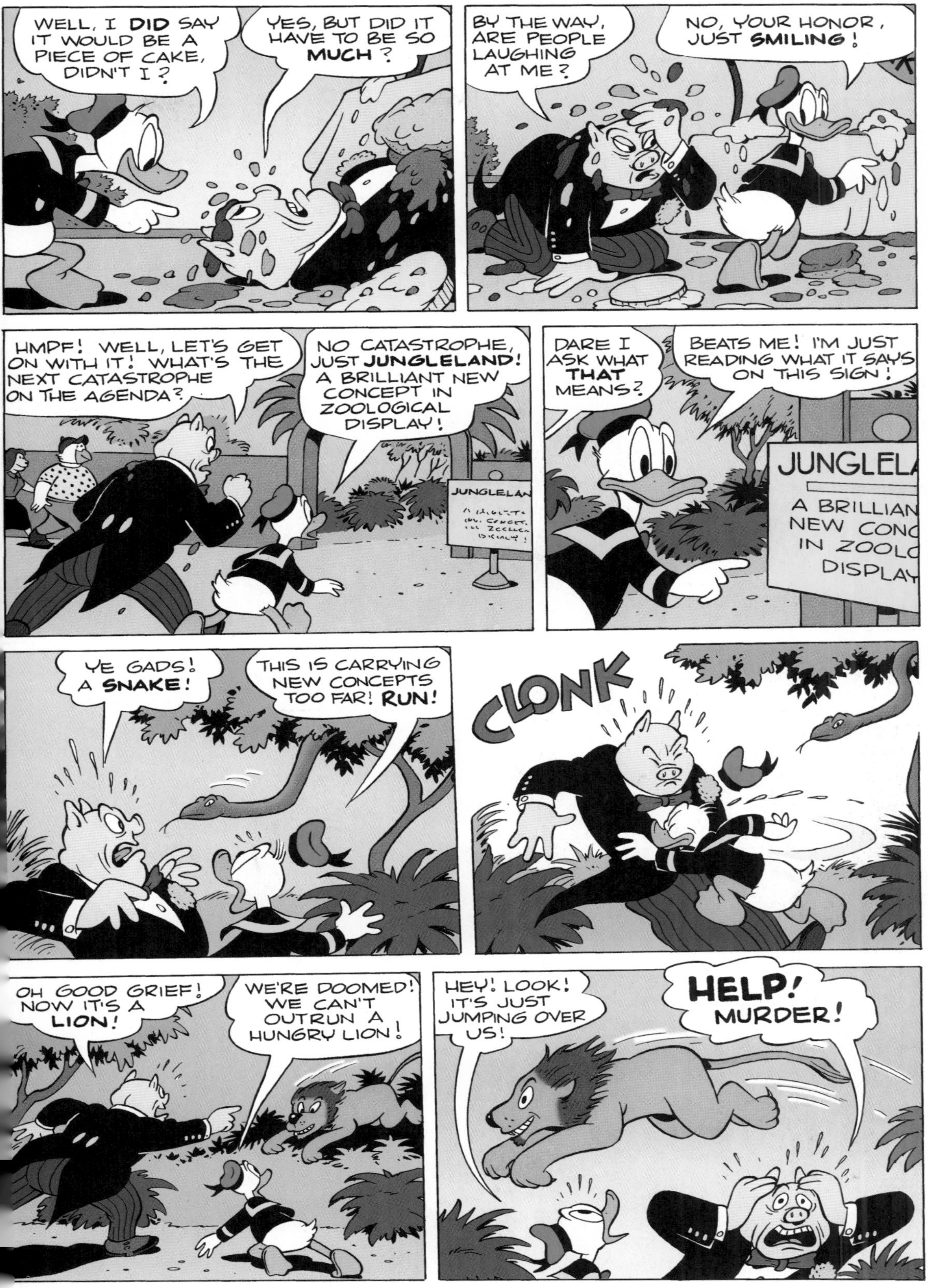

WELL, I DID SAY IT WOULD BE A PIECE OF CAKE, DIDN'T I?
YES, BUT DID IT HAVE TO BE SO MUCH?
BY THE WAY, ARE PEOPLE LAUGHING AT ME?
NO, YOUR HONOR, JUST SMILING!
HMPF! WELL, LET'S GET ON WITH IT! WHAT'S THE NEXT CATASTROPHE ON THE AGENDA?
NO CATASTROPHE, JUST JUNGLELAND! A BRILLIANT NEW CONCEPT IN ZOOLOGICAL DISPLAY!
DARE I ASK WHAT THAT MEANS?
BEATS ME! I'M JUST READING WHAT IT SAYS ON THIS SIGN!
JUNGLELA
A BRILLIAN
NEW CONC
IN ZOOLO
DISPLAY
YE GADS! A SNAKE!
THIS IS CARRYING NEW CONCEPTS TOO FAR! RUN!
CLONK
OH GOOD GRIEF! NOW IT'S A LION!
WE'RE DOOMED! WE CAN'T OUTRUN A HUNGRY LION!
HEY! LOOK! IT'S JUST JUMPING OVER US!
HELP! MURDER!

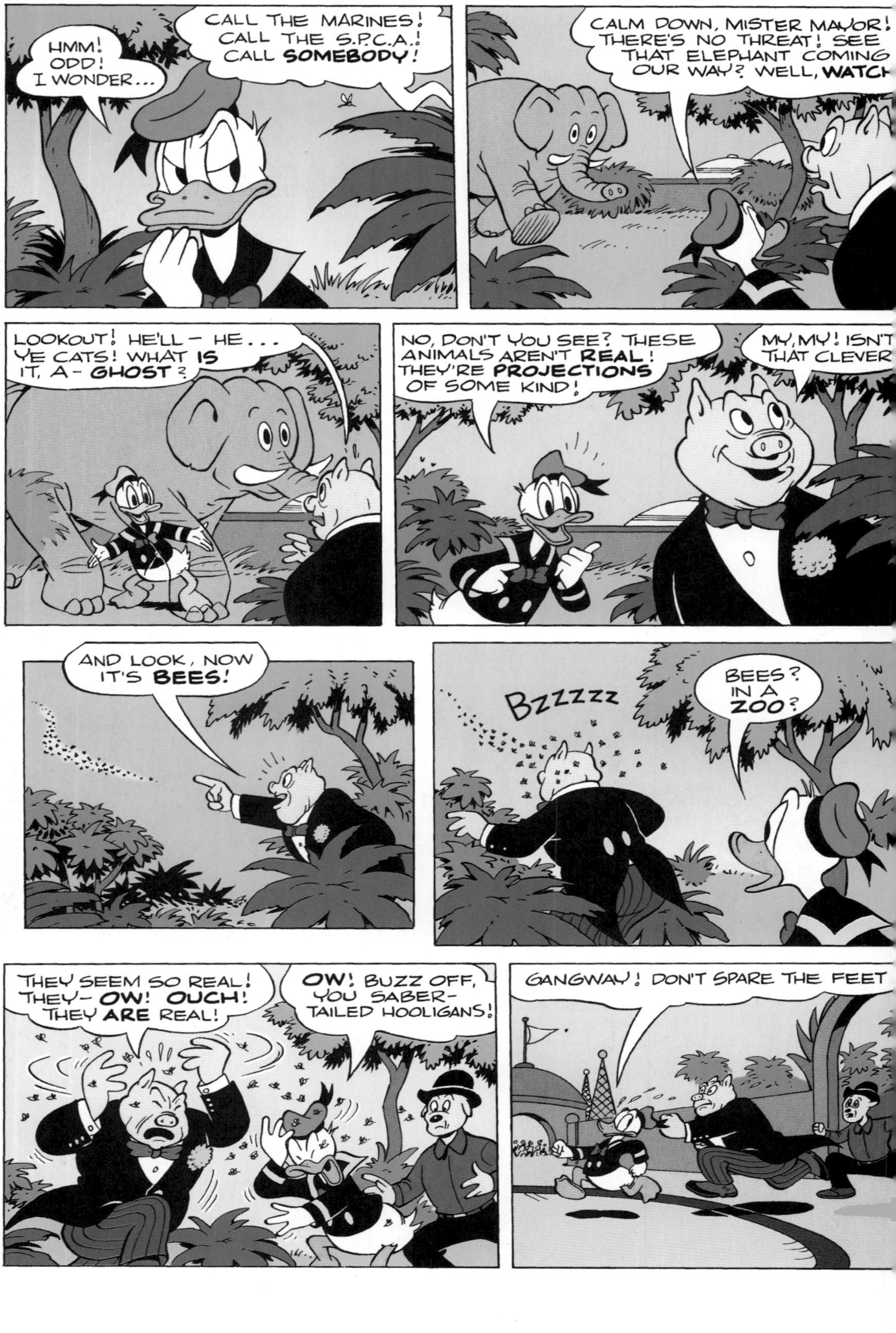
HMM! ODD! I WONDER...
CALL THE MARINES! CALL THE S.P.C.A.! CALL SOMEBODY!
CALM DOWN, MISTER MAYOR! THERE'S NO THREAT! SEE THAT ELEPHANT COMING OUR WAY? WELL, WATCH
LOOKOUT! HE'LL - HE... YE CATS! WHAT IS IT, A- GHOST?
NO, DON'T YOU SEE? THESE ANIMALS AREN'T REAL! THEY'RE PROJECTIONS OF SOME KIND!
MY, MY! ISN'T THAT CLEVER
AND LOOK, NOW IT'S BEES!
BZZZZZ
BEES? IN A ZOO?
THEY SEEM SO REAL! THEY- OW! OUCH! THEY ARE REAL!
OW! BUZZ OFF, YOU SABER-TAILED HOOLIGANS!
GANGWAY! DON'T SPARE THE FEET

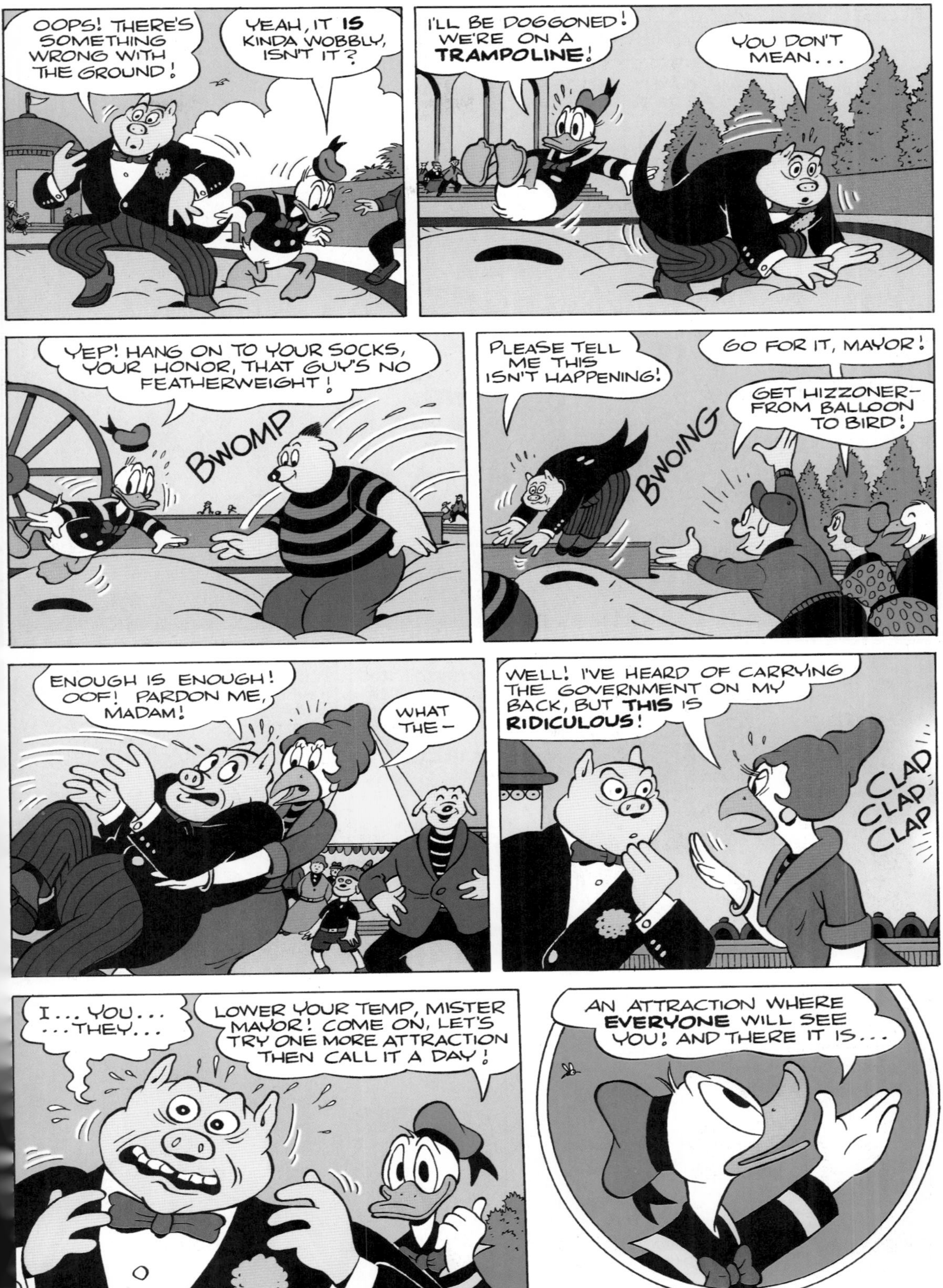
OOPS! THERE'S SOMETHING WRONG WITH THE GROUND!
YEAH, IT IS KINDA WOBBLY, ISN'T IT?
I'LL BE DOGGONED! WE'RE ON A TRAMPOLINE!
YOU DON'T MEAN...
YEP! HANG ON TO YOUR SOCKS, YOUR HONOR, THAT GUY'S NO FEATHERWEIGHT!
BWOMP
PLEASE TELL ME THIS ISN'T HAPPENING!
GO FOR IT, MAYOR!
GET HIZZONER— FROM BALLOON TO BIRD!
BWOING
ENOUGH IS ENOUGH! OOF! PARDON ME, MADAM!
WHAT THE—
WELL! I'VE HEARD OF CARRYING THE GOVERNMENT ON MY BACK, BUT THIS IS RIDICULOUS!
CLAP CLAP CLAP
I... YOU... ...THEY...
LOWER YOUR TEMP, MISTER MAYOR! COME ON, LET'S TRY ONE MORE ATTRACTION THEN CALL IT A DAY!
AN ATTRACTION WHERE EVERYONE WILL SEE YOU! AND THERE IT IS...

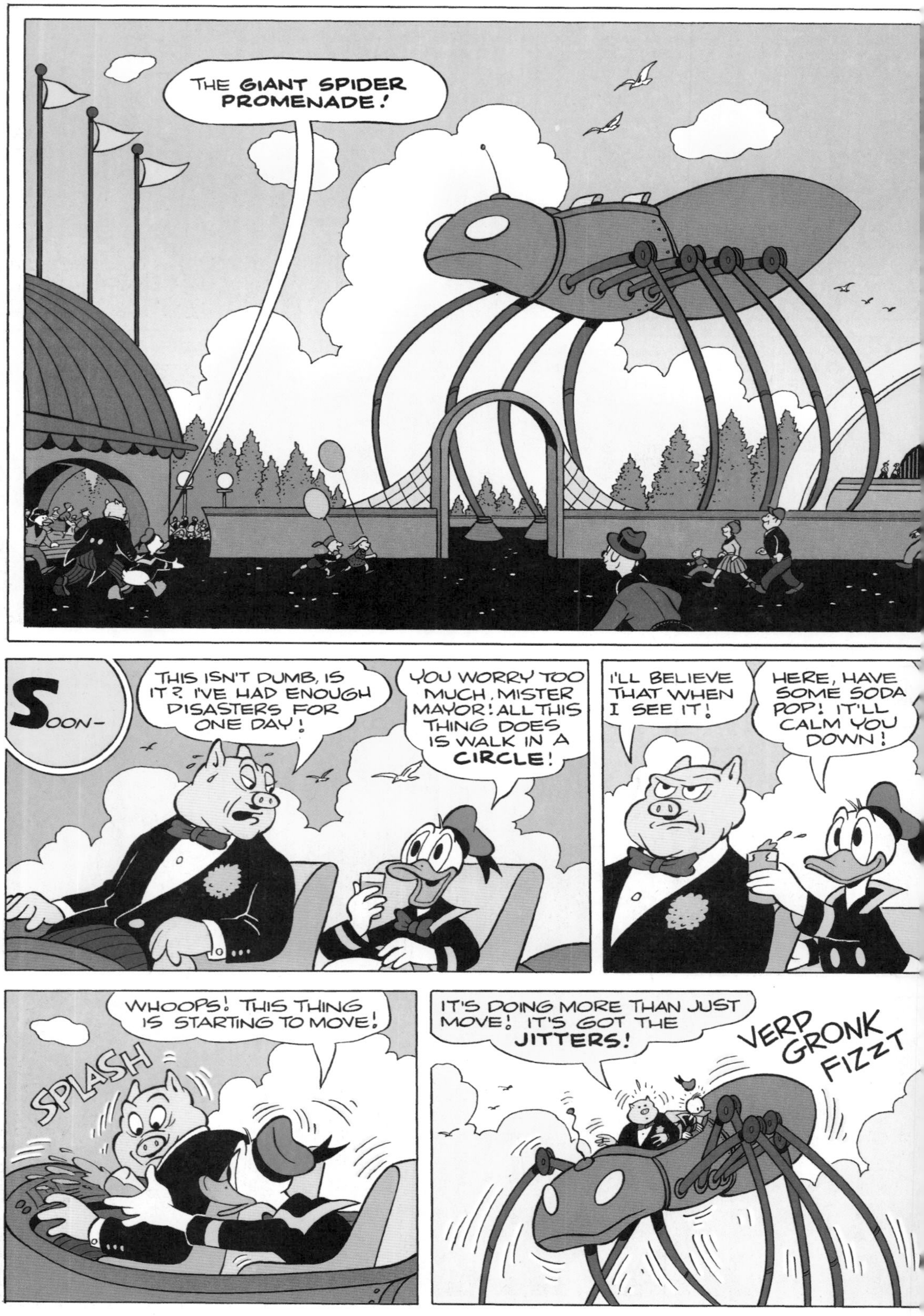
THE GIANT SPIDER PROMENADE!
SOON-
THIS ISN'T DUMB, IS IT? I'VE HAD ENOUGH DISASTERS FOR ONE DAY!
YOU WORRY TOO MUCH, MISTER MAYOR! ALL THIS THING DOES IS WALK IN A CIRCLE!
I'LL BELIEVE THAT WHEN I SEE IT!
HERE, HAVE SOME SODA POP! IT'LL CALM YOU DOWN!
WHOOPS! THIS THING IS STARTING TO MOVE!
SPLASH
IT'S DOING MORE THAN JUST MOVE! IT'S GOT THE JITTERS!
VERP
GRONK
FIZZT

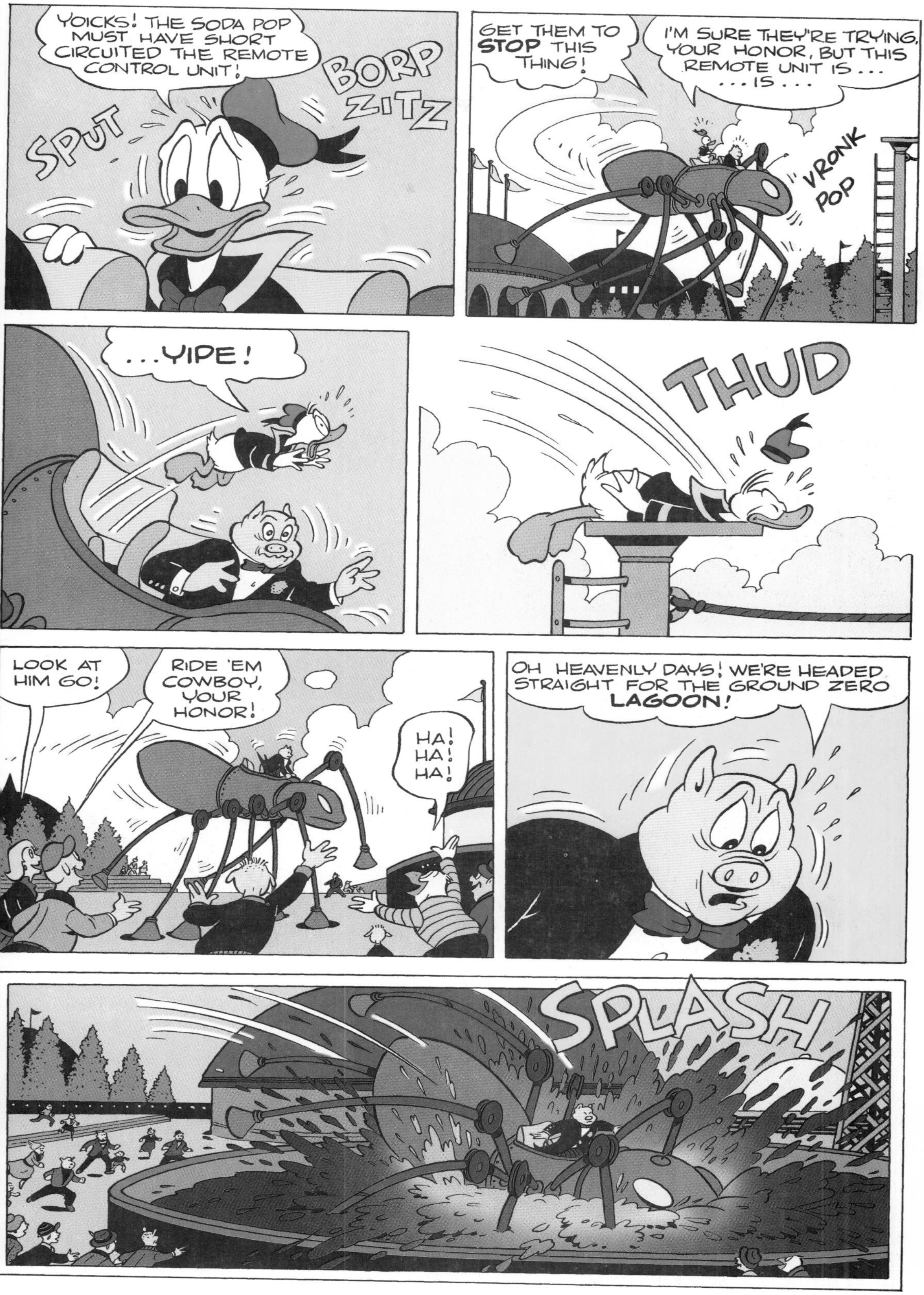
YOICKS! THE SODA POP MUST HAVE SHORT CIRCUITED THE REMOTE CONTROL UNIT!
SPUT
BORP
ZITZ
GET THEM TO STOP THIS THING!
I'M SURE THEY'RE TRYING, YOUR HONOR, BUT THIS REMOTE UNIT IS . . . . . . IS . . .
VRONK
POP
. . . YIPE!
THUD
LOOK AT HIM GO!
RIDE 'EM COWBOY, YOUR HONOR!
HA! HA! HA!
OH HEAVENLY DAYS! WE'RE HEADED STRAIGHT FOR THE GROUND ZERO LAGOON!
SPLASH

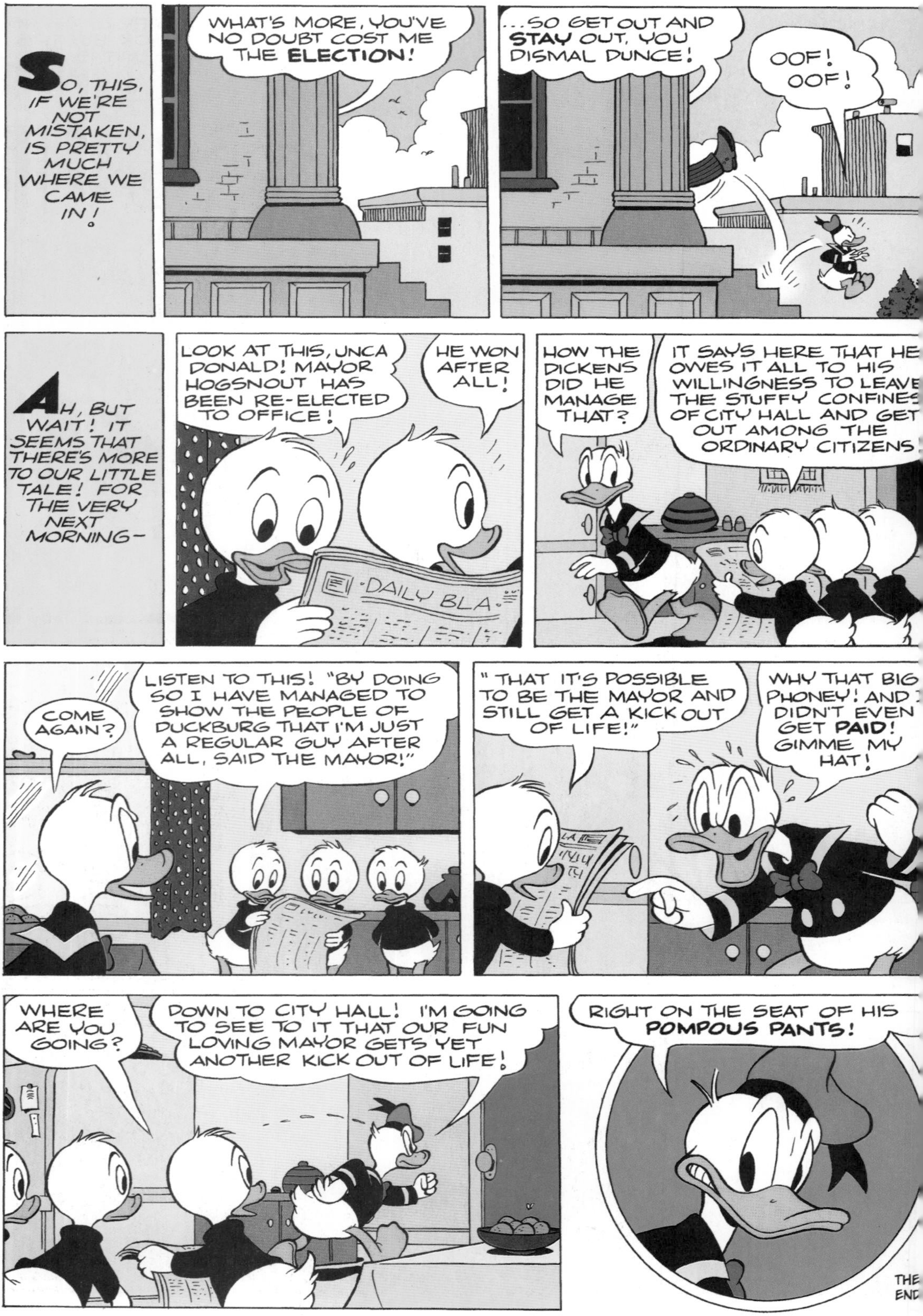
SO, THIS, IF WE'RE NOT MISTAKEN, IS PRETTY MUCH WHERE WE CAME IN!
WHAT'S MORE, YOU'VE NO DOUBT COST ME THE ELECTION!
...SO GET OUT AND STAY OUT, YOU DISMAL DUNCE!
OOF! OOF!
AH, BUT WAIT! IT SEEMS THAT THERE'S MORE TO OUR LITTLE TALE! FOR THE VERY NEXT MORNING-
LOOK AT THIS, UNCA DONALD! MAYOR HOGSNOUT HAS BEEN RE-ELECTED TO OFFICE!
HE WON AFTER ALL!
DAILY BLA
HOW THE DICKENS DID HE MANAGE THAT?
IT SAYS HERE THAT HE OWES IT ALL TO HIS WILLINGNESS TO LEAVE THE STUFFY CONFINES OF CITY HALL AND GET OUT AMONG THE ORDINARY CITIZENS!
COME AGAIN?
LISTEN TO THIS! "BY DOING SO I HAVE MANAGED TO SHOW THE PEOPLE OF DUCKBURG THAT I'M JUST A REGULAR GUY AFTER ALL, SAID THE MAYOR!"
"THAT IT'S POSSIBLE TO BE THE MAYOR AND STILL GET A KICK OUT OF LIFE!"
WHY THAT BIG PHONEY! AND I DIDN'T EVEN GET PAID! GIMME MY HAT!
WHERE ARE YOU GOING?
DOWN TO CITY HALL! I'M GOING TO SEE TO IT THAT OUR FUN LOVING MAYOR GETS YET ANOTHER KICK OUT OF LIFE!
RIGHT ON THE SEAT OF HIS POMPOUS PANTS!
THE END

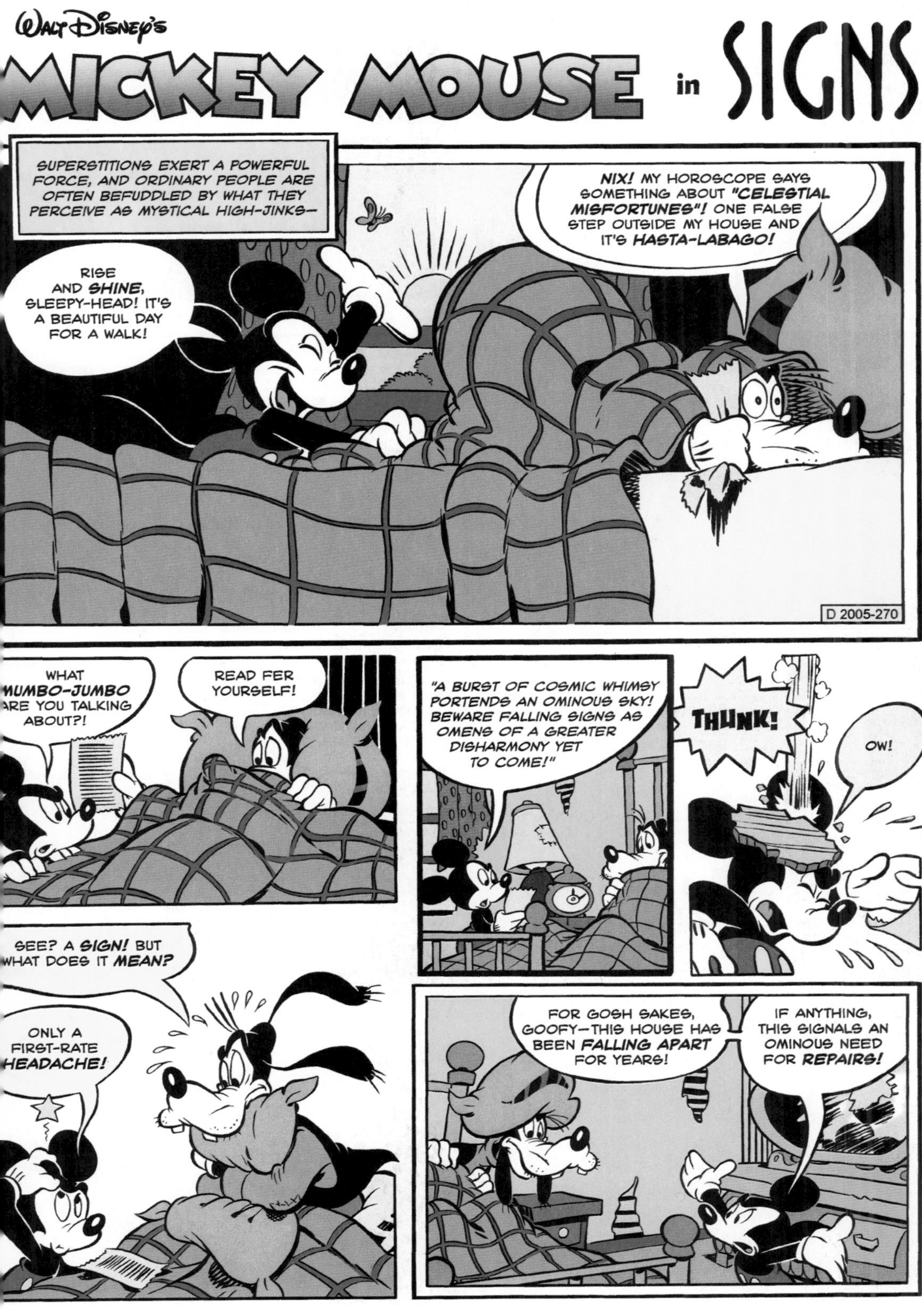
WALT DISNEY'S
MICKEY MOUSE in SIGNS
SUPERSTITIONS EXERT A POWERFUL FORCE, AND ORDINARY PEOPLE ARE OFTEN BEFUDDLED BY WHAT THEY PERCEIVE AS MYSTICAL HIGH-JINKS—
RISE AND SHINE, SLEEPY-HEAD! IT'S A BEAUTIFUL DAY FOR A WALK!
NIX! MY HOROSCOPE SAYS SOMETHING ABOUT "CELESTIAL MISFORTUNES"! ONE FALSE STEP OUTSIDE MY HOUSE AND IT'S HASTA-LABAGO!
D 2005-270
WHAT MUMBO-JUMBO ARE YOU TALKING ABOUT?!
READ FER YOURSELF!
"A BURST OF COSMIC WHIMSY PORTENDS AN OMINOUS SKY! BEWARE FALLING SIGNS AS OMENS OF A GREATER DISHARMONY YET TO COME!"
THUNK!
OW!
SEE? A SIGN! BUT WHAT DOES IT MEAN?
ONLY A FIRST-RATE HEADACHE!
FOR GOSH SAKES, GOOFY—THIS HOUSE HAS BEEN FALLING APART FOR YEARS!
IF ANYTHING, THIS SIGNALS AN OMINOUS NEED FOR REPAIRS!

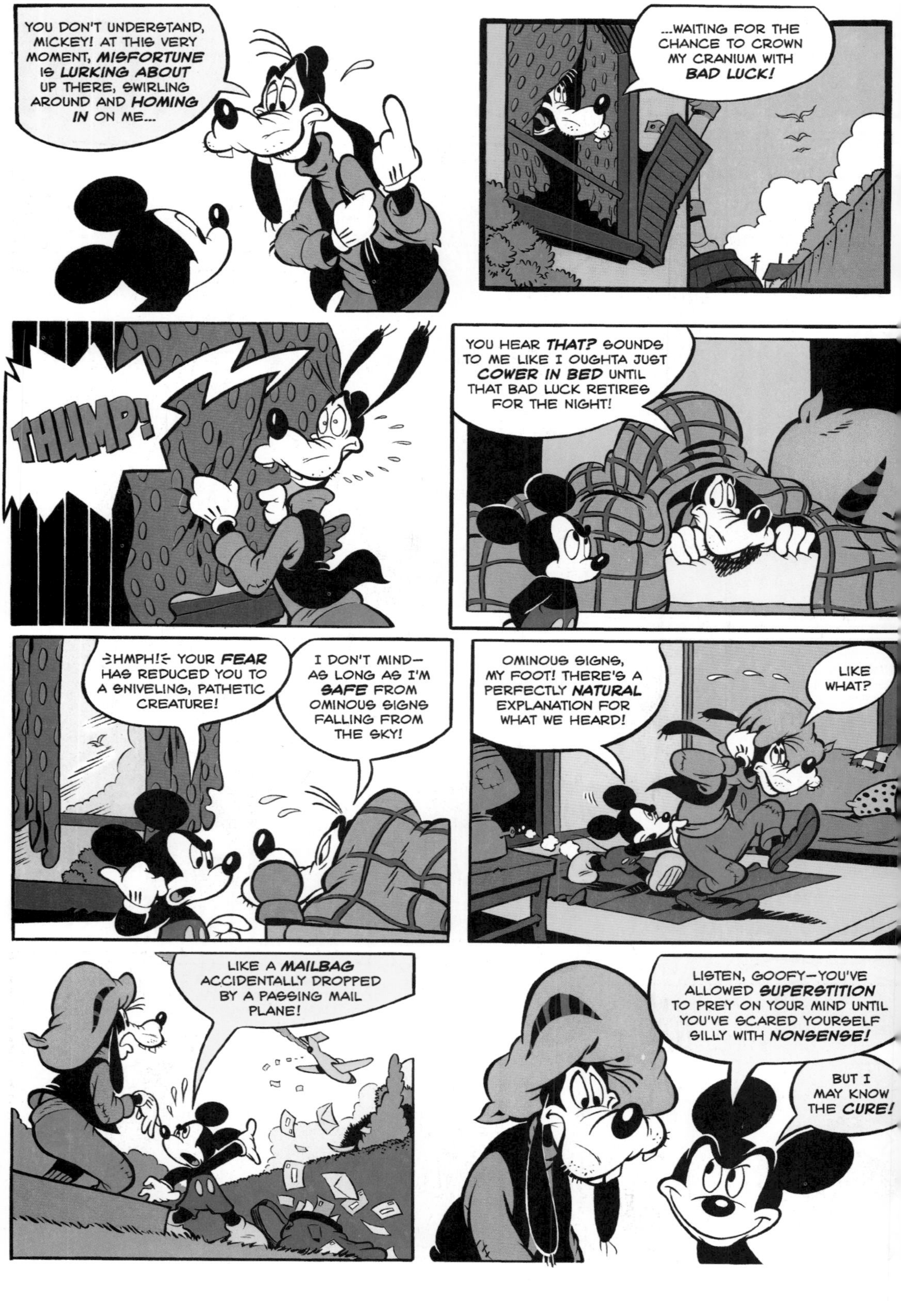
YOU DON'T UNDERSTAND, MICKEY! AT THIS VERY MOMENT, MISFORTUNE IS LURKING ABOUT UP THERE, SWIRLING AROUND AND HOMING IN ON ME...
...WAITING FOR THE CHANCE TO CROWN MY CRANIUM WITH BAD LUCK!
THUMP!
YOU HEAR THAT? SOUNDS TO ME LIKE I OUGHTA JUST COWER IN BED UNTIL THAT BAD LUCK RETIRES FOR THE NIGHT!
HMPH! YOUR FEAR HAS REDUCED YOU TO A SNIVELING, PATHETIC CREATURE!
I DON'T MIND— AS LONG AS I'M SAFE FROM OMINOUS SIGNS FALLING FROM THE SKY!
OMINOUS SIGNS, MY FOOT! THERE'S A PERFECTLY NATURAL EXPLANATION FOR WHAT WE HEARD!
LIKE WHAT?
LIKE A MAILBAG ACCIDENTALLY DROPPED BY A PASSING MAIL PLANE!
LISTEN, GOOFY—YOU'VE ALLOWED SUPERSTITION TO PREY ON YOUR MIND UNTIL YOU'VE SCARED YOURSELF SILLY WITH NONSENSE!
BUT I MAY KNOW THE CURE!

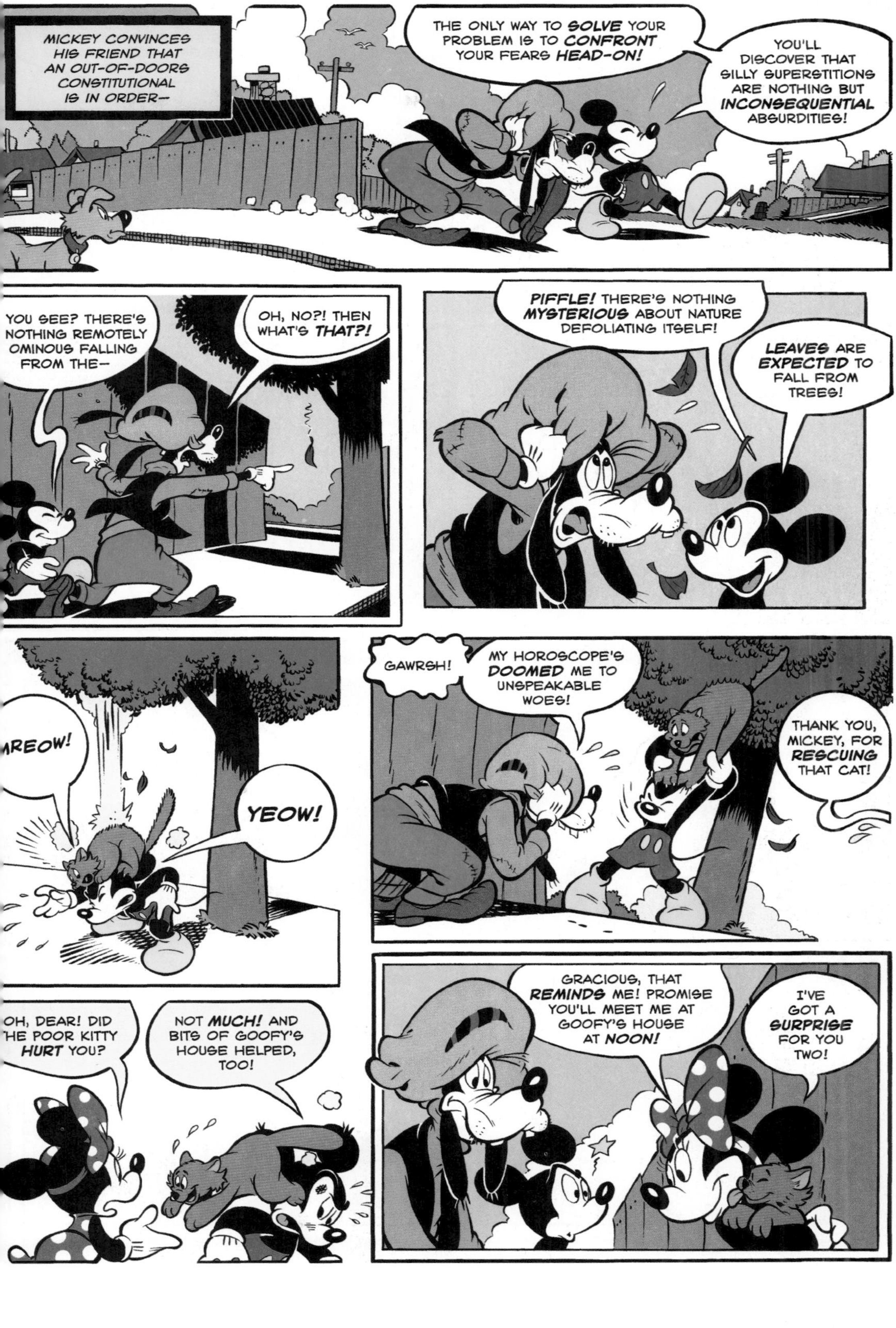

MICKEY CONVINCES HIS FRIEND THAT AN OUT-OF-DOORS CONSTITUTIONAL IS IN ORDER—
THE ONLY WAY TO SOLVE YOUR PROBLEM IS TO CONFRONT YOUR FEARS HEAD-ON!
YOU'LL DISCOVER THAT SILLY SUPERSTITIONS ARE NOTHING BUT INCONSEQUENTIAL ABSURDITIES!
YOU SEE? THERE'S NOTHING REMOTELY OMINOUS FALLING FROM THE—
OH, NO?! THEN WHAT'S THAT?!
PIFFLE! THERE'S NOTHING MYSTERIOUS ABOUT NATURE DEFOLIATING ITSELF!
LEAVES ARE EXPECTED TO FALL FROM TREES!
MREOW!
YEOW!
GAWRSH!
MY HOROSCOPE'S DOOMED ME TO UNSPEAKABLE WOES!
THANK YOU, MICKEY, FOR RESCUING THAT CAT!
OH, DEAR! DID THE POOR KITTY HURT YOU?
NOT MUCH! AND BITS OF GOOFY'S HOUSE HELPED, TOO!
GRACIOUS, THAT REMINDS ME! PROMISE YOU'LL MEET ME AT GOOFY'S HOUSE AT NOON!
I'VE GOT A SURPRISE FOR YOU TWO!

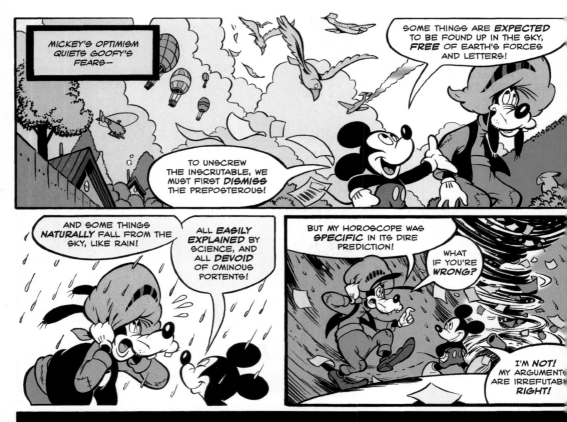

MICKEY'S OPTIMISM QUIETS GOOFY'S FEARS—

SOME THINGS ARE *EXPECTED* TO BE FOUND UP IN THE SKY, *FREE* OF EARTH'S FORCES AND LETTERS!

TO UNSCREW THE INSCRUTABLE, WE MUST FIRST *DISMISS* THE PREPOSTEROUS!

AND SOME THINGS *NATURALLY* FALL FROM THE SKY, LIKE RAIN!

ALL *EASILY EXPLAINED* BY SCIENCE, AND ALL *DEVOID* OF OMINOUS PORTENTS!

BUT MY HOROSCOPE WAS *SPECIFIC* IN ITS DIRE PREDICTION!

WHAT IF YOU'RE *WRONG?*

I'M *NOT!* MY ARGUMENTS ARE IRREFUTABLY *RIGHT!*

OR MAYBE *UNRIGHT*, MR. SMARTY-PANTS!

RELAX, GOOFY! THERE'S ABSOLUTELY *NOTHING* MYSTERIOUS OR OMINOUS ABOUT THIS! IN FACT, I *EXPECTED* IT TO HAPPEN!

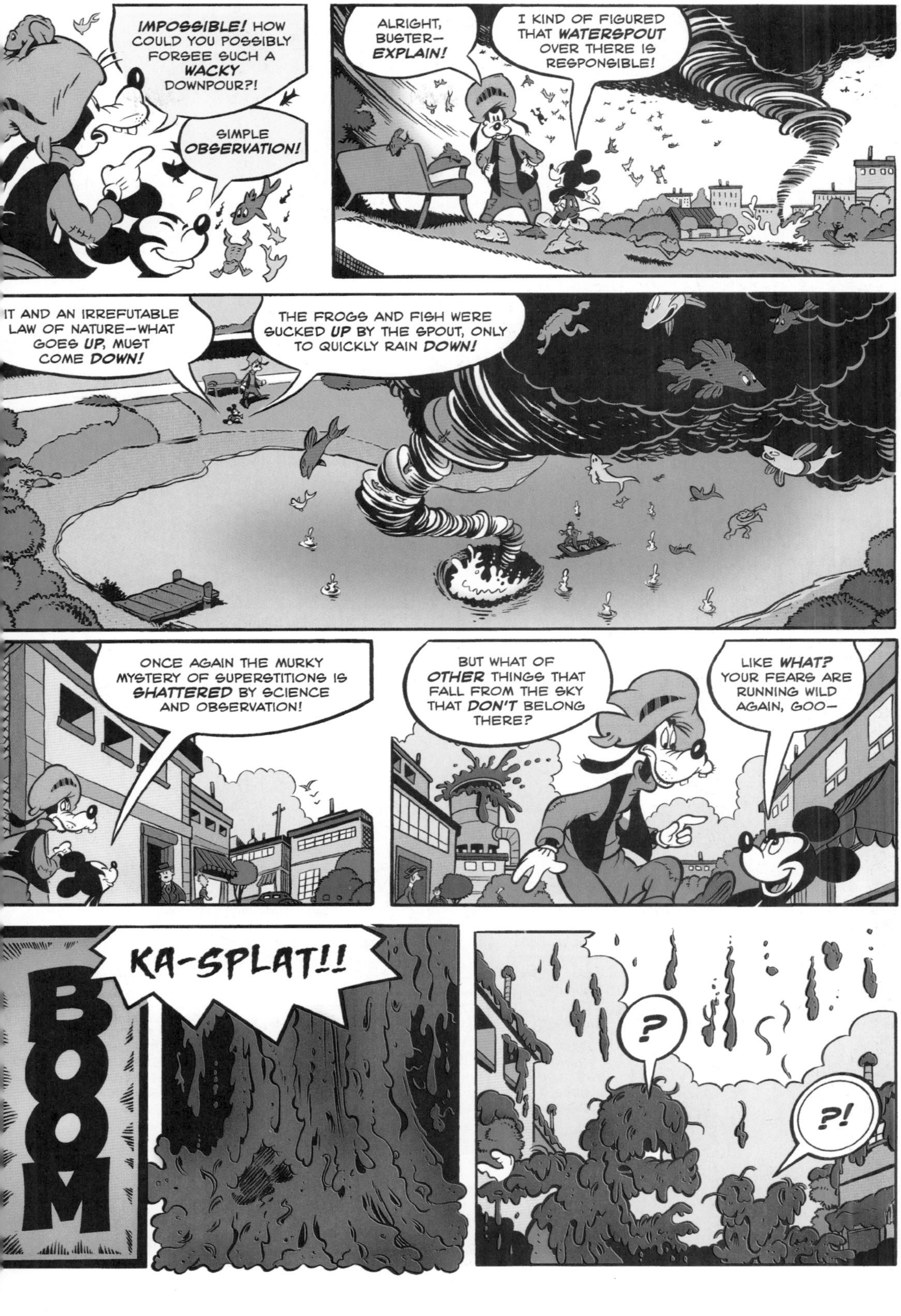

IMPOSSIBLE! HOW COULD YOU POSSIBLY FORSEE SUCH A WACKY DOWNPOUR?!
SIMPLE OBSERVATION!
ALRIGHT, BUSTER— EXPLAIN!
I KIND OF FIGURED THAT WATERSPOUT OVER THERE IS RESPONSIBLE!
IT AND AN IRREFUTABLE LAW OF NATURE—WHAT GOES UP, MUST COME DOWN!
THE FROGS AND FISH WERE SUCKED UP BY THE SPOUT, ONLY TO QUICKLY RAIN DOWN!
ONCE AGAIN THE MURKY MYSTERY OF SUPERSTITIONS IS SHATTERED BY SCIENCE AND OBSERVATION!
BUT WHAT OF OTHER THINGS THAT FALL FROM THE SKY THAT DON'T BELONG THERE?
LIKE WHAT? YOUR FEARS ARE RUNNING WILD AGAIN, GOO—
BOOM
KA-SPLAT!!
?
?!

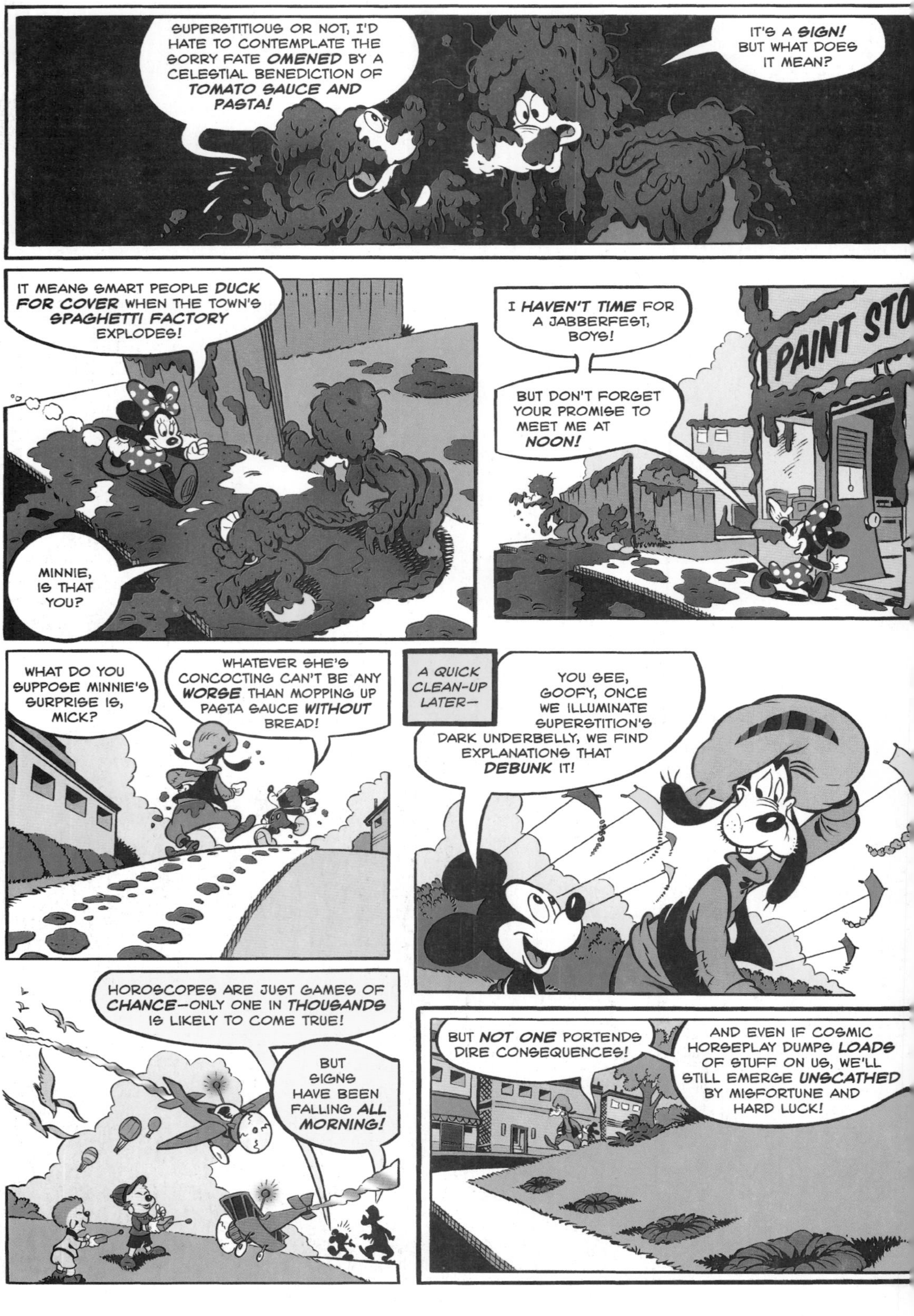
SUPERSTITIOUS OR NOT, I'D HATE TO CONTEMPLATE THE SORRY FATE **OMENED** BY A CELESTIAL BENEDICTION OF **TOMATO SAUCE AND PASTA!**
IT'S A **SIGN!** BUT WHAT DOES IT MEAN?
IT MEANS SMART PEOPLE **DUCK FOR COVER** WHEN THE TOWN'S **SPAGHETTI FACTORY** EXPLODES!
MINNIE, IS THAT YOU?
I **HAVEN'T TIME** FOR A JABBERFEST, BOYS!
BUT DON'T FORGET YOUR PROMISE TO MEET ME AT **NOON!**
PAINT STO
WHAT DO YOU SUPPOSE MINNIE'S SURPRISE IS, MICK?
WHATEVER SHE'S CONCOCTING CAN'T BE ANY **WORSE** THAN MOPPING UP PASTA SAUCE **WITHOUT** BREAD!
A QUICK CLEAN-UP LATER—
YOU SEE, GOOFY, ONCE WE ILLUMINATE SUPERSTITION'S DARK UNDERBELLY, WE FIND EXPLANATIONS THAT **DEBUNK** IT!
HOROSCOPES ARE JUST GAMES OF **CHANCE**—ONLY ONE IN **THOUSANDS** IS LIKELY TO COME TRUE!
BUT SIGNS HAVE BEEN FALLING **ALL MORNING!**
BUT **NOT ONE** PORTENDS DIRE CONSEQUENCES!
AND EVEN IF COSMIC HORSEPLAY DUMPS **LOADS** OF STUFF ON US, WE'LL STILL EMERGE **UNSCATHED** BY MISFORTUNE AND HARD LUCK!

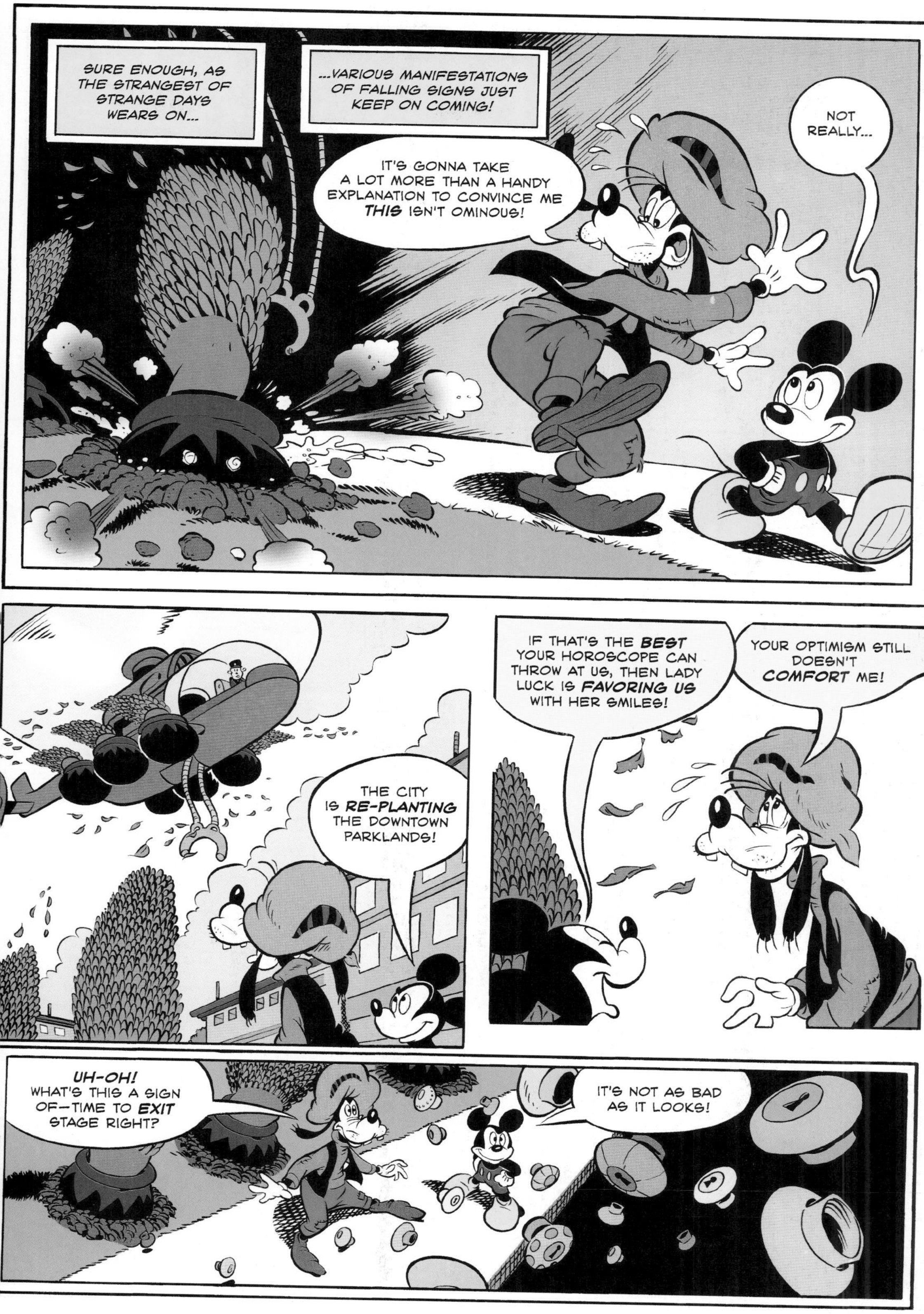
SURE ENOUGH, AS THE STRANGEST OF STRANGE DAYS WEARS ON...
...VARIOUS MANIFESTATIONS OF FALLING SIGNS JUST KEEP ON COMING!
IT'S GONNA TAKE A LOT MORE THAN A HANDY EXPLANATION TO CONVINCE ME THIS ISN'T OMINOUS!
NOT REALLY...
THE CITY IS RE-PLANTING THE DOWNTOWN PARKLANDS!
IF THAT'S THE BEST YOUR HOROSCOPE CAN THROW AT US, THEN LADY LUCK IS FAVORING US WITH HER SMILES!
YOUR OPTIMISM STILL DOESN'T COMFORT ME!
UH-OH! WHAT'S THIS A SIGN OF—TIME TO EXIT STAGE RIGHT?
IT'S NOT AS BAD AS IT LOOKS!

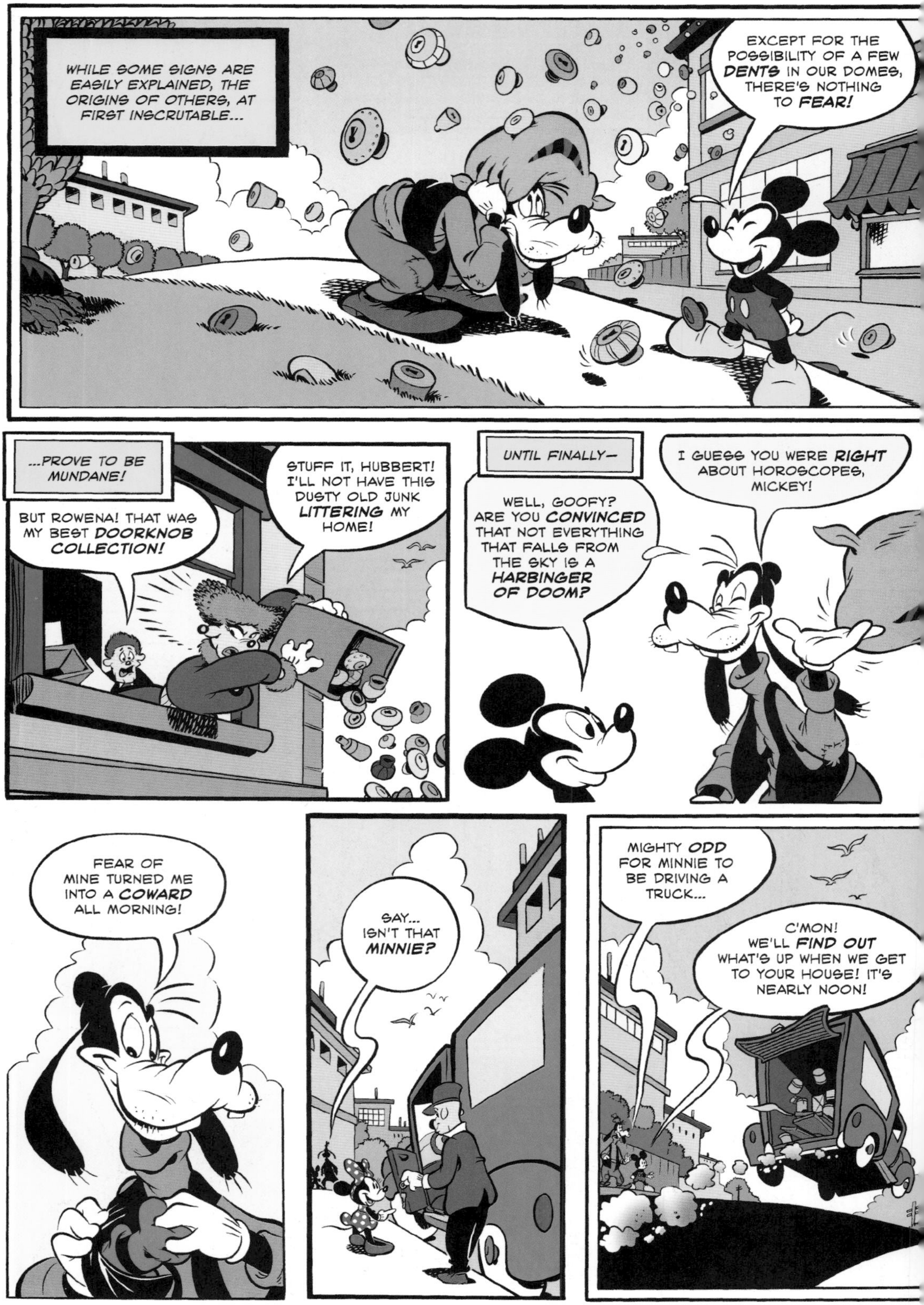
WHILE SOME SIGNS ARE EASILY EXPLAINED, THE ORIGINS OF OTHERS, AT FIRST INSCRUTABLE...
EXCEPT FOR THE POSSIBILITY OF A FEW DENTS IN OUR DOMES, THERE'S NOTHING TO FEAR!
...PROVE TO BE MUNDANE!
BUT ROWENA! THAT WAS MY BEST DOORKNOB COLLECTION!
STUFF IT, HUBBERT! I'LL NOT HAVE THIS DUSTY OLD JUNK LITTERING MY HOME!
UNTIL FINALLY—
WELL, GOOFY? ARE YOU CONVINCED THAT NOT EVERYTHING THAT FALLS FROM THE SKY IS A HARBINGER OF DOOM?
I GUESS YOU WERE RIGHT ABOUT HOROSCOPES, MICKEY!
FEAR OF MINE TURNED ME INTO A COWARD ALL MORNING!
SAY... ISN'T THAT MINNIE?
MIGHTY ODD FOR MINNIE TO BE DRIVING A TRUCK...
C'MON! WE'LL FIND OUT WHAT'S UP WHEN WE GET TO YOUR HOUSE! IT'S NEARLY NOON!

GAWRSH, MICK—AREN'T YOU A *TEENSY* BIT SUPERSTITIOUS?

I'M NOT AFRAID OF *IGNORANCE*, GOOFY!

BUT I DO POSSES ONE *ANXIETY* THAT LIES *DEEP* BENEATH THE SURFACE, *SECRET*, HIDDEN FROM MORTAL EYES!

YEAH? *WHAT?*

GETTING *ROPED INTO* ANOTHER ONE OF MINNIE'S *PET PROJECTS!*

MY BRAIN *SHRIVELS* AT THE VERY THOUGHT OF CHARITY BAKE SALES AND CLOTHING HOMELESS PIGEONS!

ANYTHING SHE VOLUNTEERS ME TO DO!

HA! AREN'T YOUR FEARS MORE LIKELY TO *COME TRUE* THAN MINE?

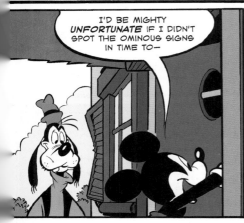

I'D BE MIGHTY *UNFORTUNATE* IF I DIDN'T SPOT THE OMINOUS SIGNS IN TIME TO—

THUNK! SMASH!

?!

DOGGONE IT, GOOFY! WHY DON'T YOU *FIX* THIS HOUSE? IT'S FALLING DOWN AROUND MY EARS!

MICKEY MOUSE! YOU *SPOILED* MY *SURPRISE!*

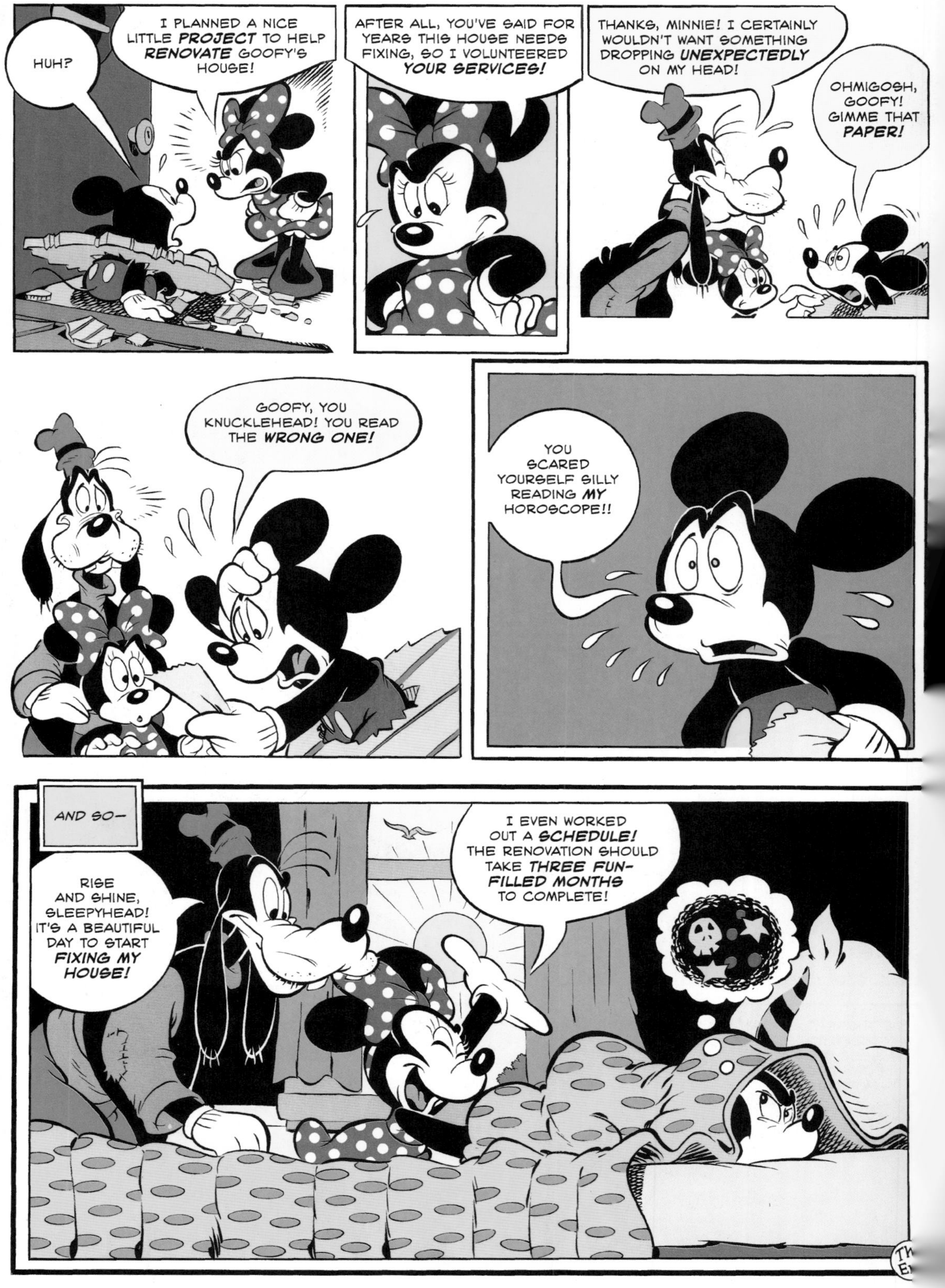
HUH?
I PLANNED A NICE LITTLE **PROJECT** TO HELP **RENOVATE** GOOFY'S HOUSE!
AFTER ALL, YOU'VE SAID FOR YEARS THIS HOUSE NEEDS FIXING, SO I VOLUNTEERED **YOUR SERVICES!**
THANKS, MINNIE! I CERTAINLY WOULDN'T WANT SOMETHING DROPPING **UNEXPECTEDLY** ON MY HEAD!
OHMIGOSH, GOOFY! GIMME THAT **PAPER!**
GOOFY, YOU KNUCKLEHEAD! YOU READ THE **WRONG ONE!**
YOU SCARED YOURSELF SILLY READING **MY** HOROSCOPE!!
AND SO—
RISE AND SHINE, SLEEPYHEAD! IT'S A BEAUTIFUL DAY TO START **FIXING MY HOUSE!**
I EVEN WORKED OUT A **SCHEDULE!** THE RENOVATION SHOULD TAKE **THREE FUN-FILLED MONTHS** TO COMPLETE!

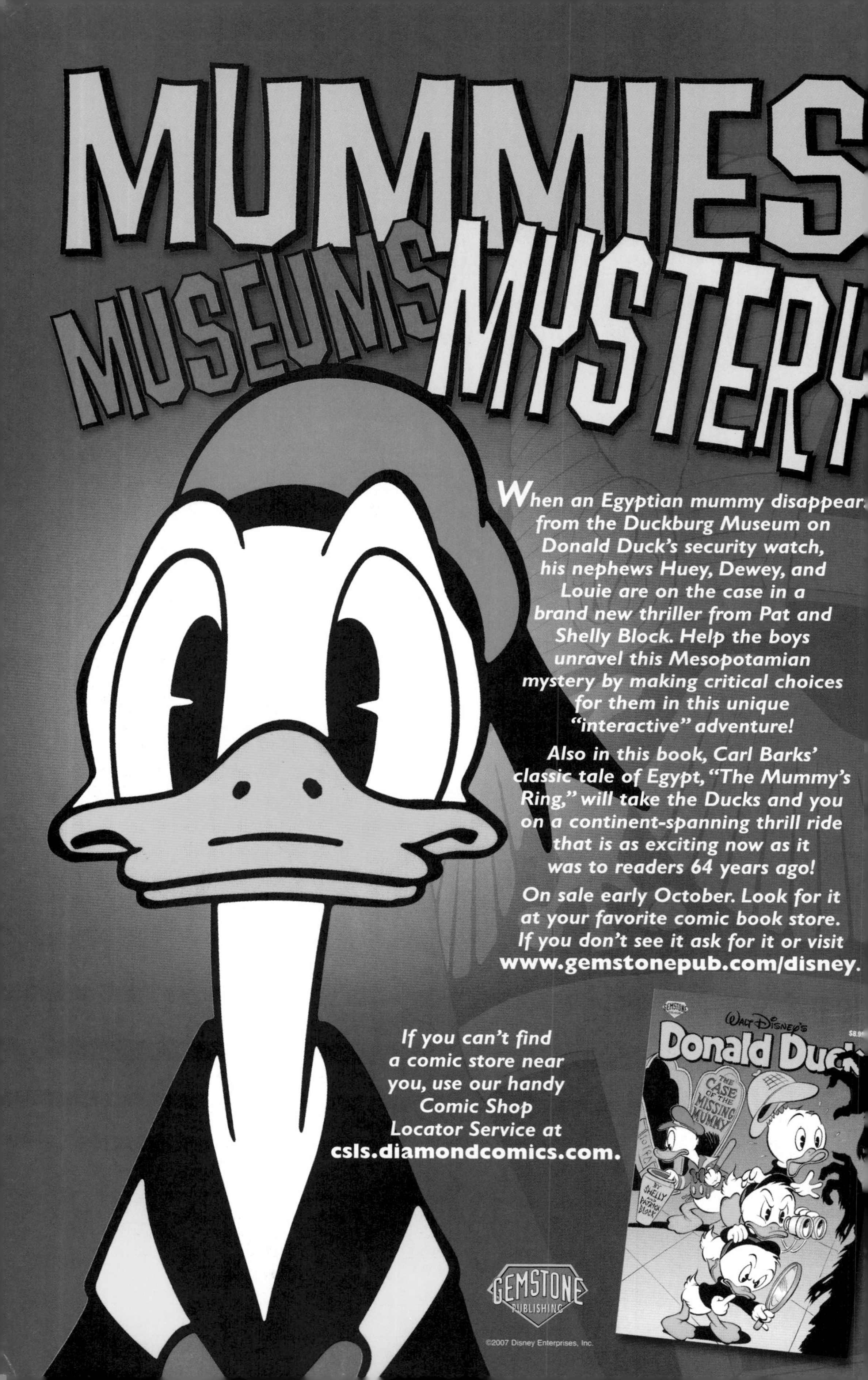
MUMMIES
MUSEUMS
MYSTERY
When an Egyptian mummy disappears from the Duckburg Museum on Donald Duck's security watch, his nephews Huey, Dewey, and Louie are on the case in a brand new thriller from Pat and Shelly Block. Help the boys unravel this Mesopotamian mystery by making critical choices for them in this unique "interactive" adventure!
Also in this book, Carl Barks' classic tale of Egypt, "The Mummy's Ring," will take the Ducks and you on a continent-spanning thrill ride that is as exciting now as it was to readers 64 years ago!
On sale early October. Look for it at your favorite comic book store. If you don't see it ask for it or visit www.gemstonepub.com/disney.
Walt Disney's
Donald Duck
The Case of the Missing Mummy
By Shelly and Patrick Block
If you can't find a comic store near you, use our handy Comic Shop Locator Service at csls.diamondcomics.com.
Gemstone Publishing
©2007 Disney Enterprises, Inc.

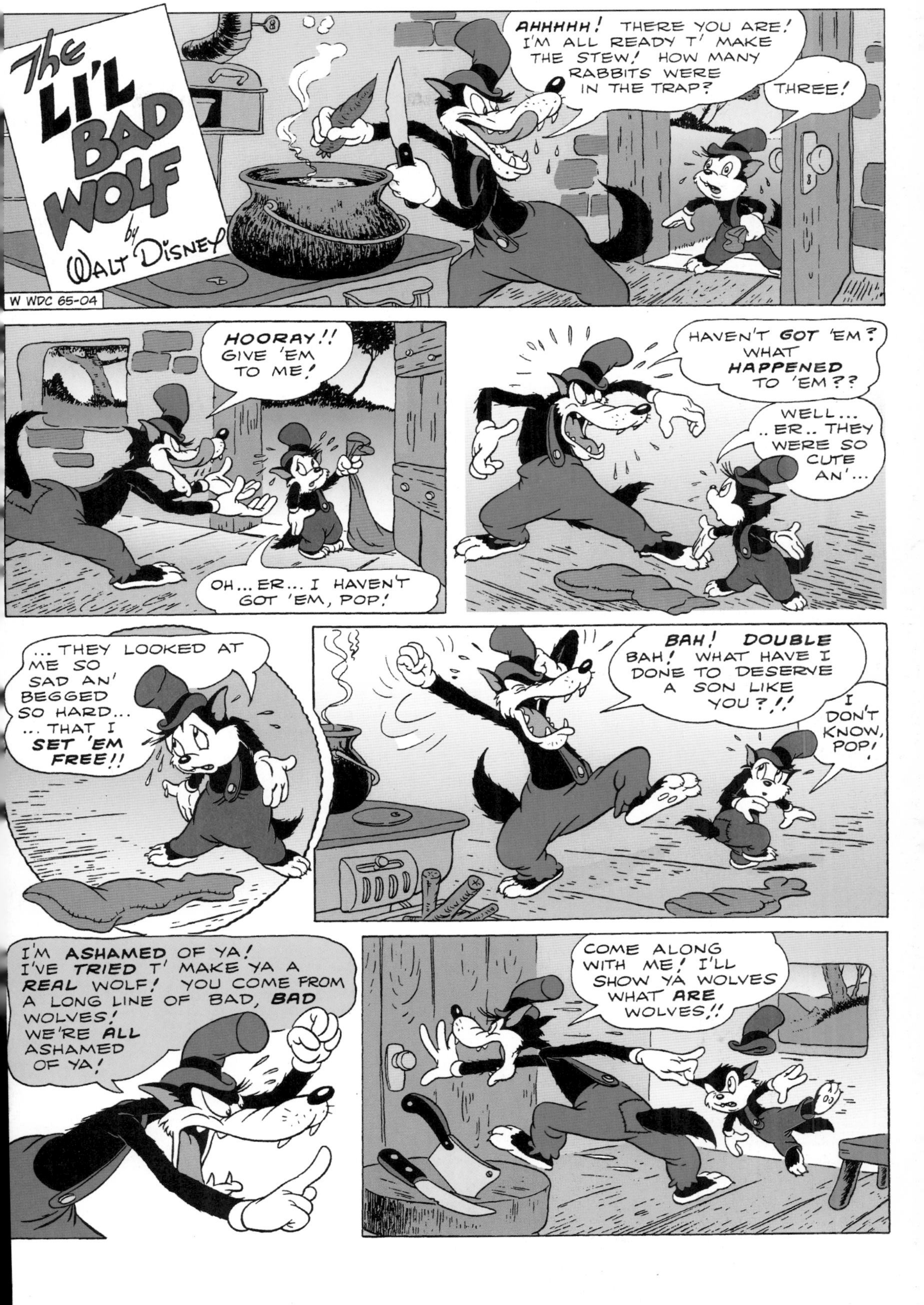

The LI'L BAD WOLF by WALT DISNEY
W WDC 65-04
AHHHHH! THERE YOU ARE! I'M ALL READY T' MAKE THE STEW! HOW MANY RABBITS WERE IN THE TRAP?
THREE!
HOORAY!! GIVE 'EM TO ME!
OH... ER... I HAVEN'T GOT 'EM, POP!
HAVEN'T GOT 'EM? WHAT HAPPENED TO 'EM??
WELL... ..ER.. THEY WERE SO CUTE AN'...
... THEY LOOKED AT ME SO SAD AN' BEGGED SO HARD... ... THAT I SET 'EM FREE!!
BAH! DOUBLE BAH! WHAT HAVE I DONE TO DESERVE A SON LIKE YOU?!!
I DON'T KNOW, POP!
I'M ASHAMED OF YA! I'VE TRIED T' MAKE YA A REAL WOLF! YOU COME FROM A LONG LINE OF BAD, BAD WOLVES! WE'RE ALL ASHAMED OF YA!
COME ALONG WITH ME! I'LL SHOW YA WOLVES WHAT ARE WOLVES!!

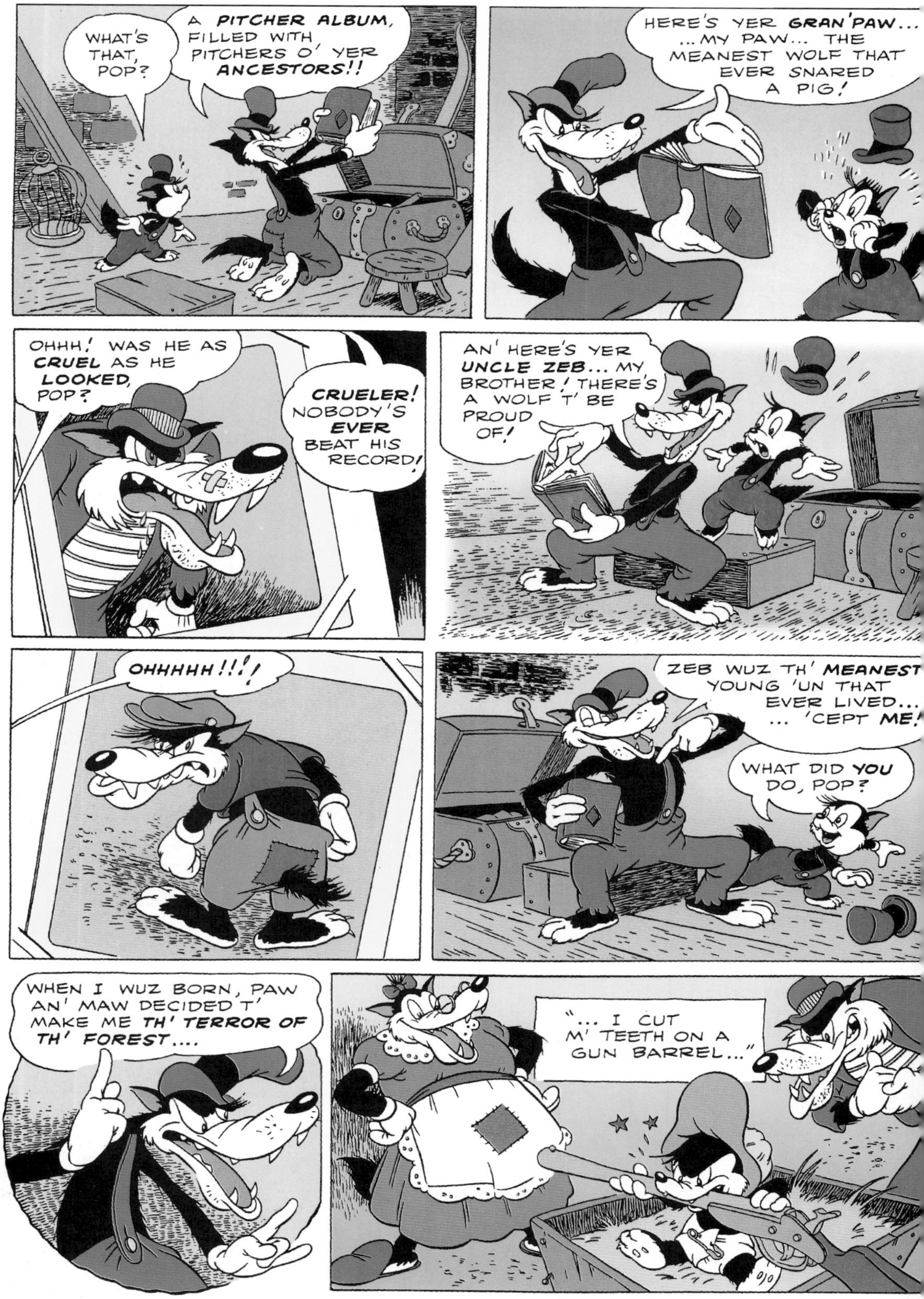
WHAT'S THAT, POP?
A PITCHER ALBUM, FILLED WITH PITCHERS O' YER ANCESTORS!!
HERE'S YER GRAN'PAW... ...MY PAW... THE MEANEST WOLF THAT EVER SNARED A PIG!
OHHH! WAS HE AS CRUEL AS HE LOOKED, POP?
CRUELER! NOBODY'S EVER BEAT HIS RECORD!
AN' HERE'S YER UNCLE ZEB... MY BROTHER! THERE'S A WOLF T' BE PROUD OF!
OHHHHH!!!!
ZEB WUZ TH' MEANEST YOUNG 'UN THAT EVER LIVED... ... 'CEPT ME!
WHAT DID YOU DO, POP?
WHEN I WUZ BORN, PAW AN' MAW DECIDED T' MAKE ME TH' TERROR OF TH' FOREST....
"... I CUT M' TEETH ON A GUN BARREL..."

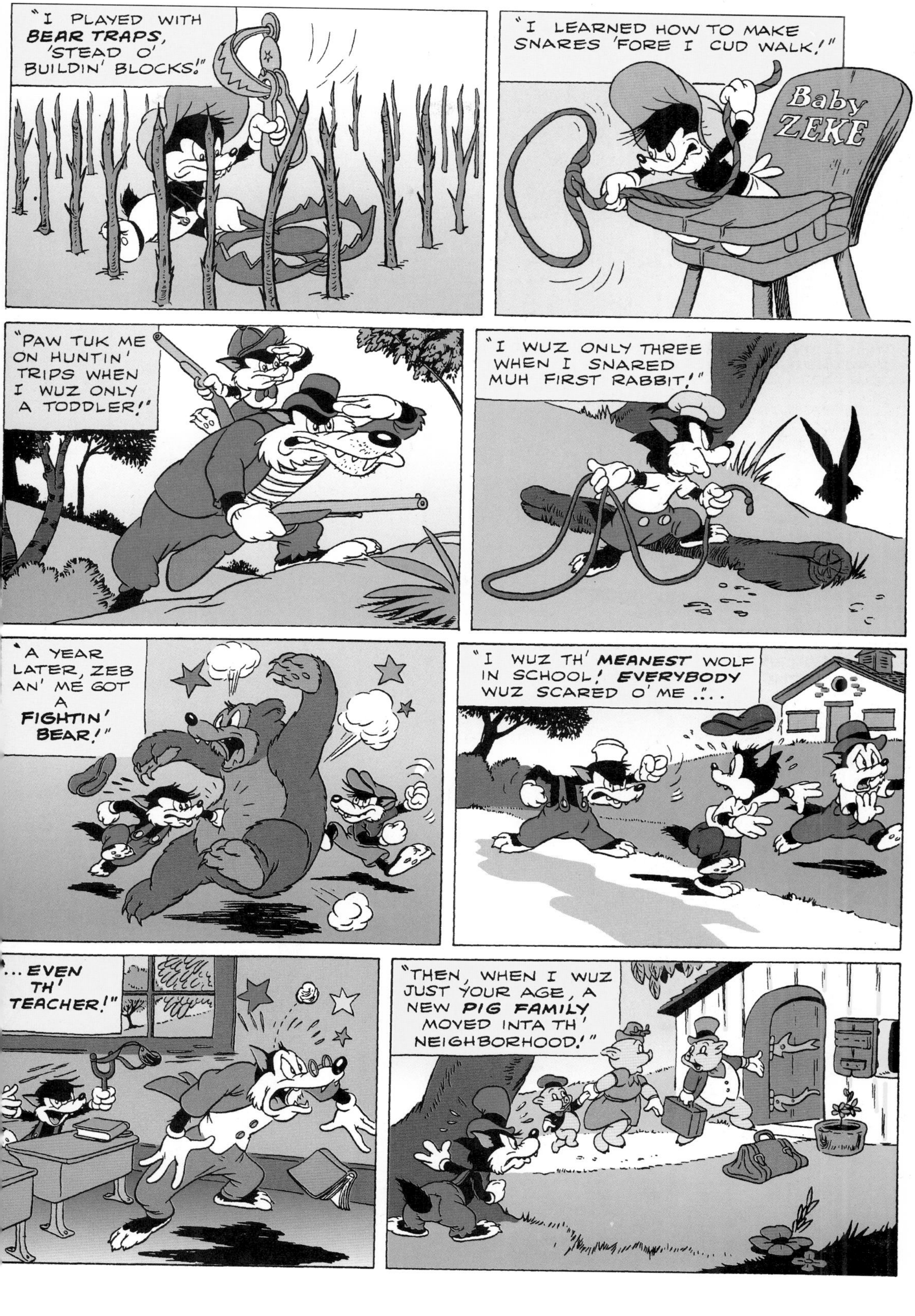
"I PLAYED WITH BEAR TRAPS, 'STEAD O' BUILDIN' BLOCKS!"
"I LEARNED HOW TO MAKE SNARES 'FORE I CUD WALK!"
Baby ZEKE
"PAW TUK ME ON HUNTIN' TRIPS WHEN I WUZ ONLY A TODDLER!"
"I WUZ ONLY THREE WHEN I SNARED MUH FIRST RABBIT!"
"A YEAR LATER, ZEB AN' ME GOT A FIGHTIN' BEAR!"
"I WUZ TH' MEANEST WOLF IN SCHOOL! EVERYBODY WUZ SCARED O' ME ..."
... EVEN TH' TEACHER!"
"THEN, WHEN I WUZ JUST YOUR AGE, A NEW PIG FAMILY MOVED INTA TH' NEIGHBORHOOD!"

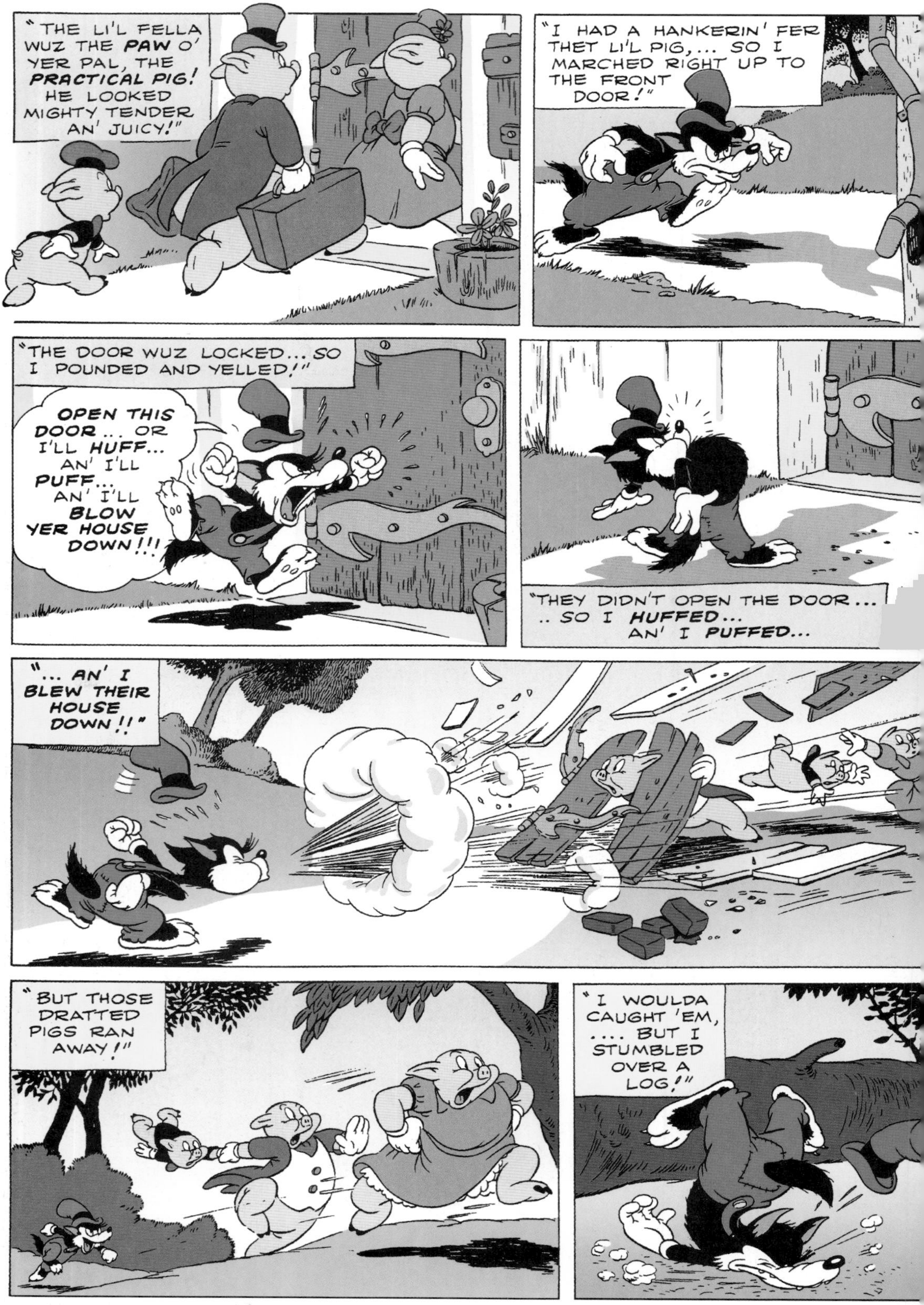

"THE LI'L FELLA WUZ THE PAW O' YER PAL, THE PRACTICAL PIG! HE LOOKED MIGHTY TENDER AN' JUICY!"
"I HAD A HANKERIN' FER THET LI'L PIG,... SO I MARCHED RIGHT UP TO THE FRONT DOOR!"
"THE DOOR WUZ LOCKED... SO I POUNDED AND YELLED!"
OPEN THIS DOOR... OR I'LL HUFF... AN' I'LL PUFF... AN' I'LL BLOW YER HOUSE DOWN!!!
"THEY DIDN'T OPEN THE DOOR... .. SO I HUFFED... AN' I PUFFED...
"... AN' I BLEW THEIR HOUSE DOWN!!"
"BUT THOSE DRATTED PIGS RAN AWAY!"
"I WOULDA CAUGHT 'EM, ... BUT I STUMBLED OVER A LOG!"

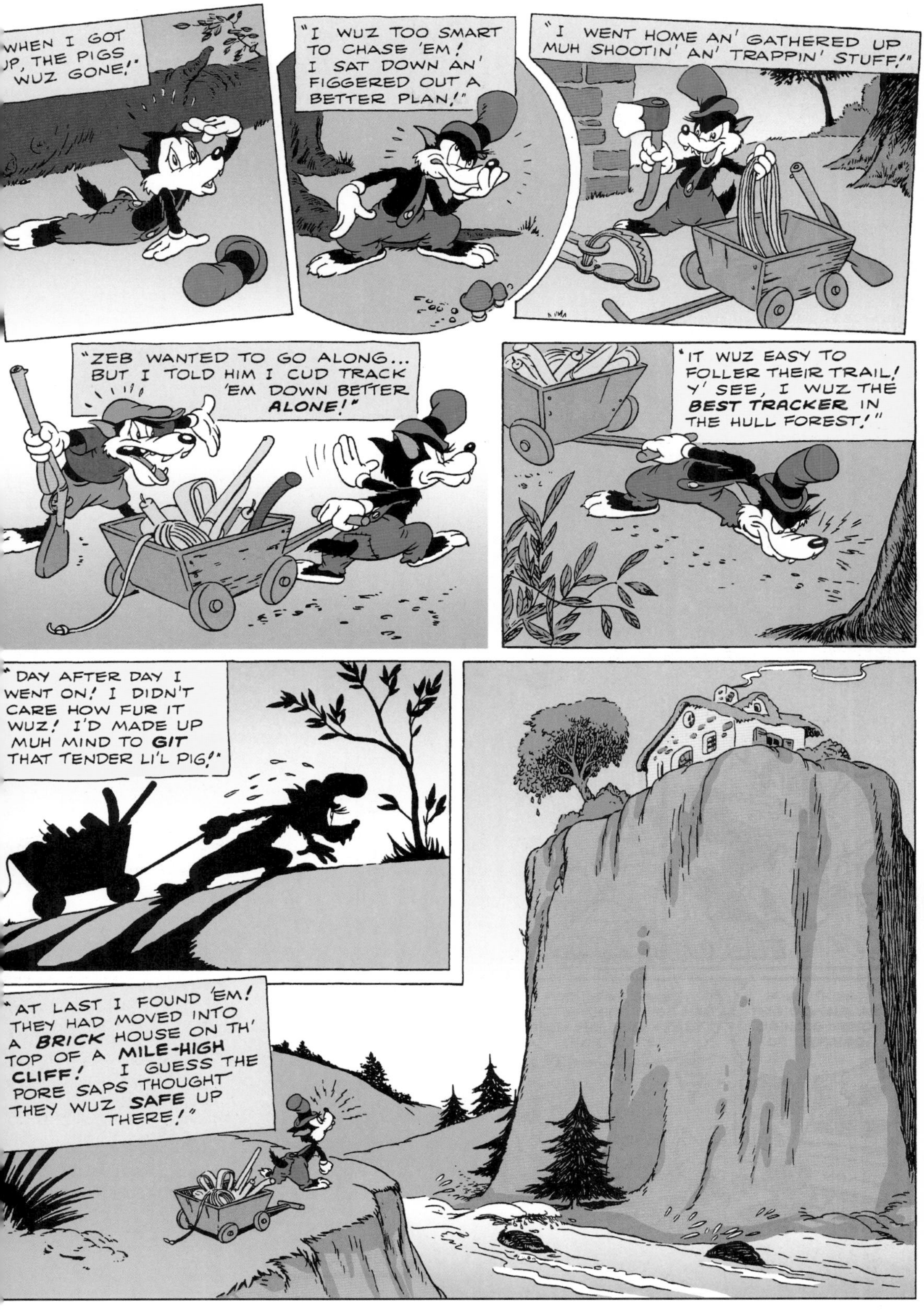
"WHEN I GOT UP, THE PIGS WUZ GONE!"
"I WUZ TOO SMART TO CHASE 'EM! I SAT DOWN AN' FIGGERED OUT A BETTER PLAN!"
"I WENT HOME AN' GATHERED UP MUH SHOOTIN' AN' TRAPPIN' STUFF!"
"ZEB WANTED TO GO ALONG... BUT I TOLD HIM I CUD TRACK 'EM DOWN BETTER ALONE!"
"IT WUZ EASY TO FOLLER THEIR TRAIL! Y' SEE, I WUZ THE BEST TRACKER IN THE HULL FOREST!"
"DAY AFTER DAY I WENT ON! I DIDN'T CARE HOW FUR IT WUZ! I'D MADE UP MUH MIND TO GIT THAT TENDER LI'L PIG!"
"AT LAST I FOUND 'EM! THEY HAD MOVED INTO A BRICK HOUSE ON TH' TOP OF A MILE-HIGH CLIFF! I GUESS THE PORE SAPS THOUGHT THEY WUZ SAFE UP THERE!"

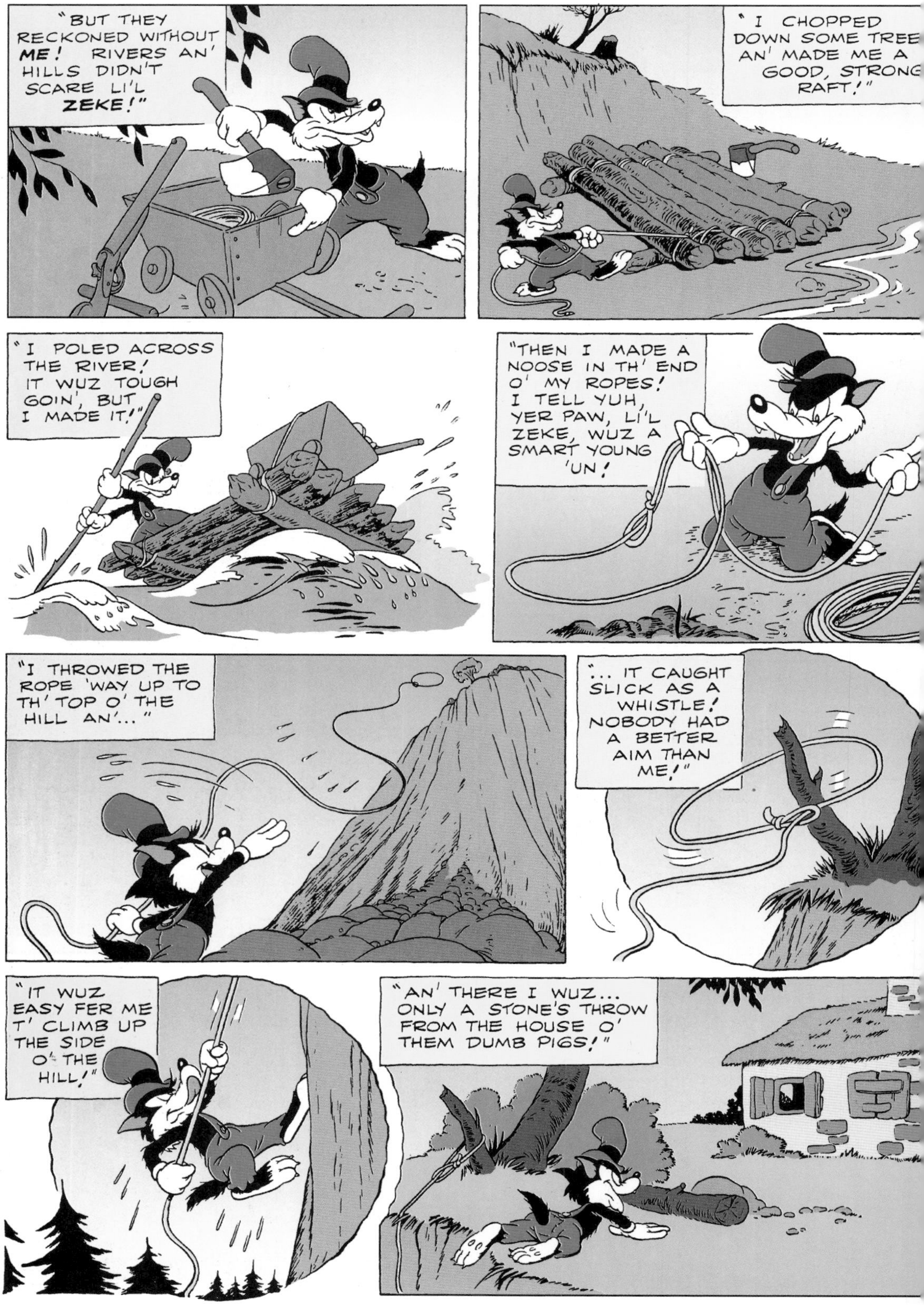
"BUT THEY RECKONED WITHOUT ME! RIVERS AN' HILLS DIDN'T SCARE LI'L ZEKE!"
"I CHOPPED DOWN SOME TREE AN' MADE ME A GOOD, STRONG RAFT!"
"I POLED ACROSS THE RIVER! IT WUZ TOUGH GOIN', BUT I MADE IT!"
"THEN I MADE A NOOSE IN TH' END O' MY ROPES! I TELL YUH, YER PAW, LI'L ZEKE, WUZ A SMART YOUNG 'UN!
"I THROWED THE ROPE 'WAY UP TO TH' TOP O' THE HILL AN'..."
"... IT CAUGHT SLICK AS A WHISTLE! NOBODY HAD A BETTER AIM THAN ME!"
"IT WUZ EASY FER ME T' CLIMB UP THE SIDE O' THE HILL!"
"AN' THERE I WUZ... ONLY A STONE'S THROW FROM THE HOUSE O' THEM DUMB PIGS!"

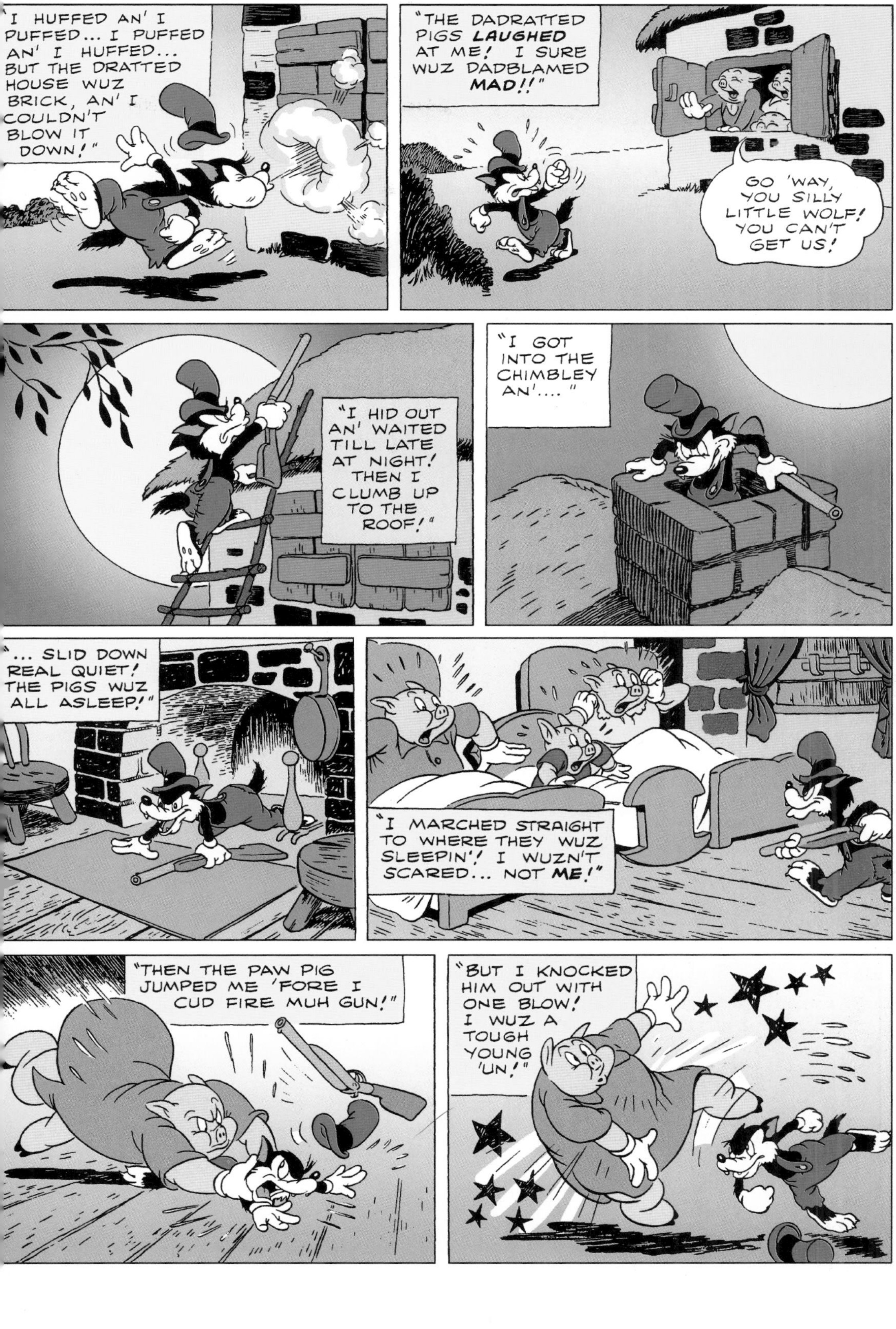
"I HUFFED AN' I PUFFED... I PUFFED AN' I HUFFED... BUT THE DRATTED HOUSE WUZ BRICK, AN' I COULDN'T BLOW IT DOWN!"
"THE DADRATTED PIGS **LAUGHED** AT ME! I SURE WUZ DADBLAMED **MAD!!**"
GO 'WAY, YOU SILLY LITTLE WOLF! YOU CAN'T GET US!
"I HID OUT AN' WAITED TILL LATE AT NIGHT! THEN I CLUMB UP TO THE ROOF!"
"I GOT INTO THE CHIMBLEY AN'...."
"... SLID DOWN REAL QUIET! THE PIGS WUZ ALL ASLEEP!"
"I MARCHED STRAIGHT TO WHERE THEY WUZ SLEEPIN'! I WUZN'T SCARED... NOT **ME!**"
"THEN THE PAW PIG JUMPED ME 'FORE I CUD FIRE MUH GUN!"
"BUT I KNOCKED HIM OUT WITH ONE BLOW! I WUZ A TOUGH YOUNG 'UN!"

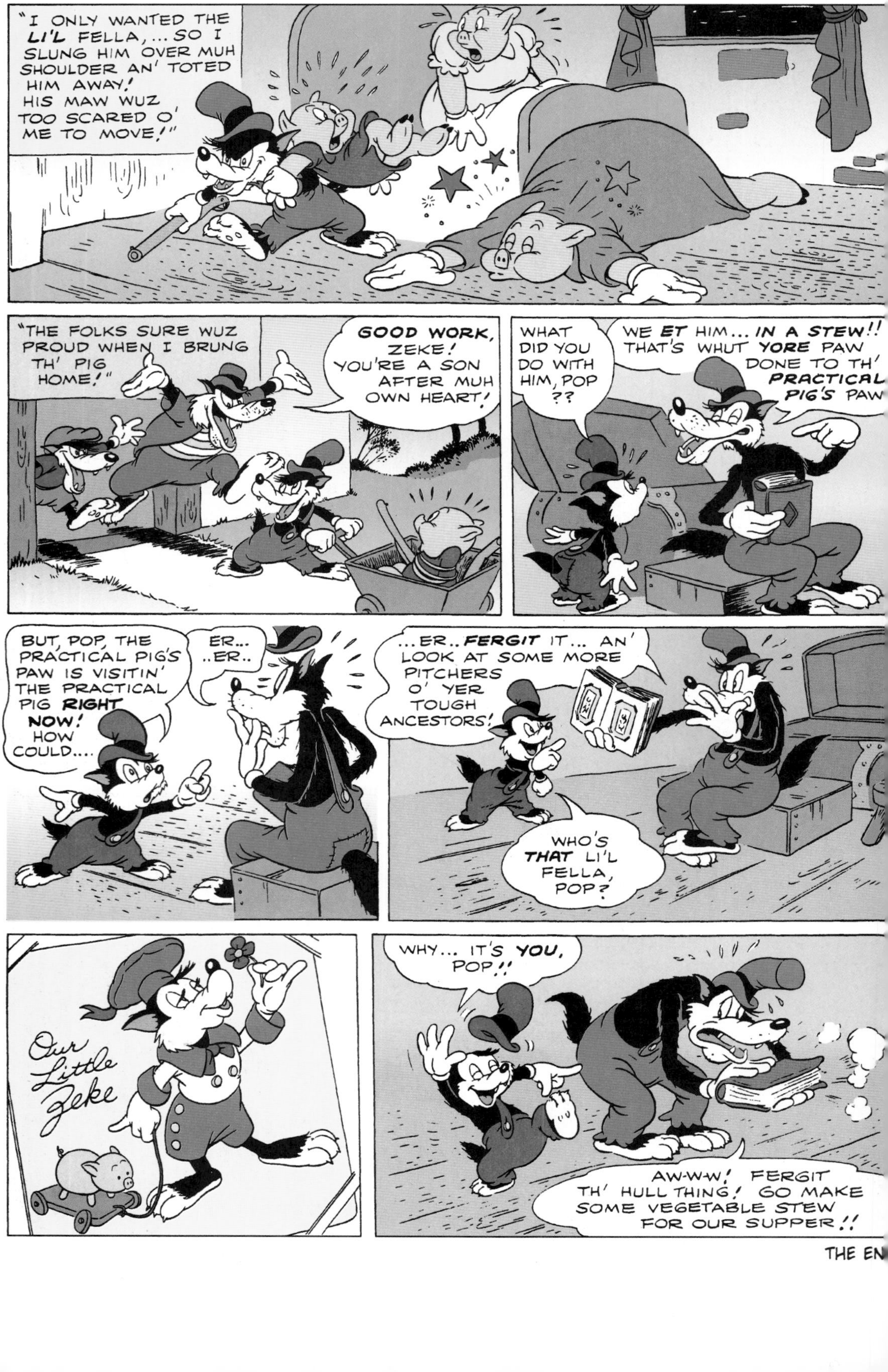
"I ONLY WANTED THE LI'L FELLA, ... SO I SLUNG HIM OVER MUH SHOULDER AN' TOTED HIM AWAY! HIS MAW WUZ TOO SCARED O' ME TO MOVE!"
"THE FOLKS SURE WUZ PROUD WHEN I BRUNG TH' PIG HOME!"
GOOD WORK, ZEKE! YOU'RE A SON AFTER MUH OWN HEART!
WHAT DID YOU DO WITH HIM, POP ??
WE ET HIM ... IN A STEW!! THAT'S WHUT YORE PAW DONE TO TH' PRACTICAL PIG'S PAW
BUT, POP, THE PRACTICAL PIG'S PAW IS VISITIN' THE PRACTICAL PIG RIGHT NOW! HOW COULD....
ER... ..ER..
...ER.. FERGIT IT... AN' LOOK AT SOME MORE PITCHERS O' YER TOUGH ANCESTORS!
WHO'S THAT LI'L FELLA, POP?
Our Little Zeke
WHY... IT'S YOU, POP!!
AW-W-W! FERGIT TH' HULL THING! GO MAKE SOME VEGETABLE STEW FOR OUR SUPPER!!
THE EN

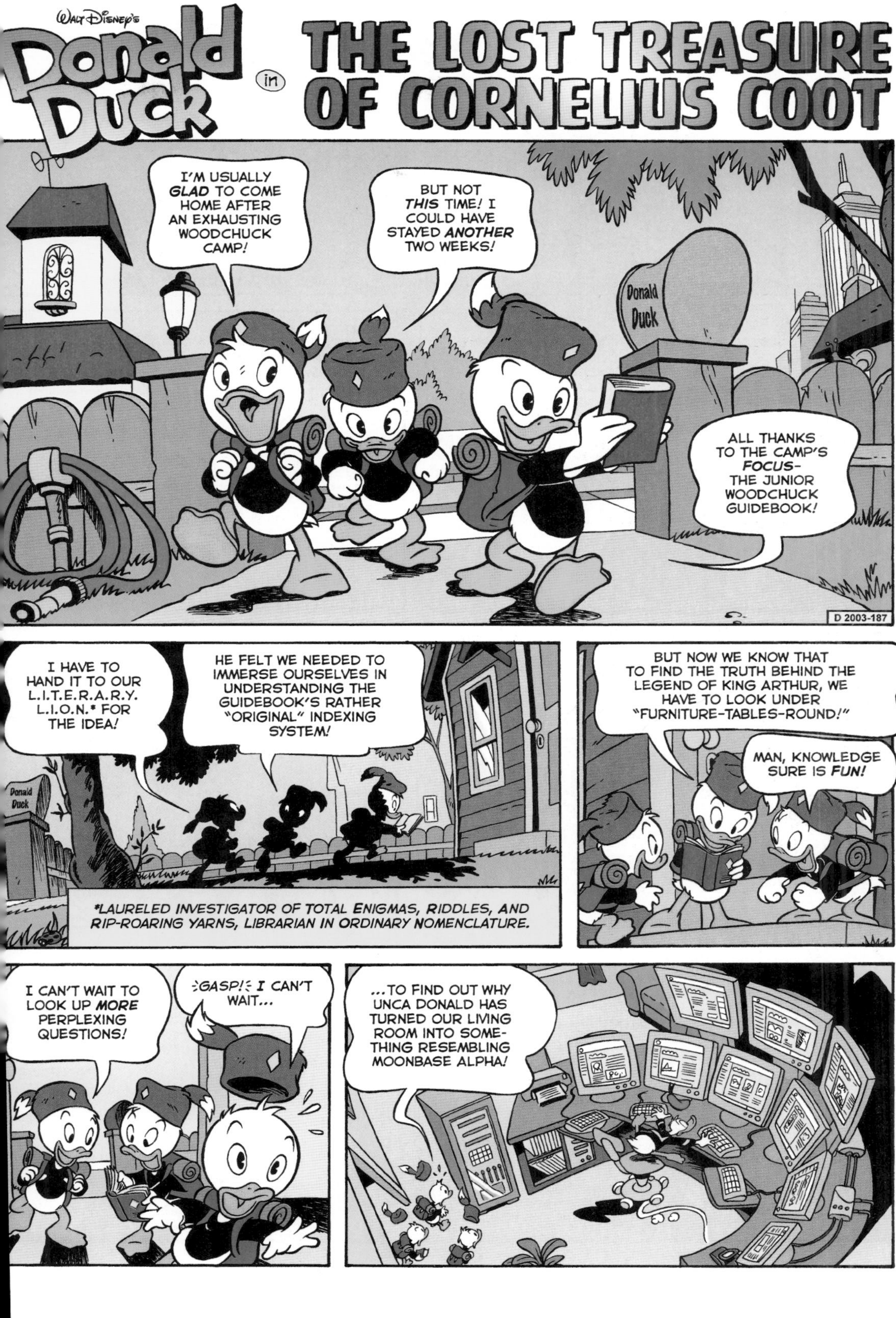
Walt Disney's
Donald Duck
in
THE LOST TREASURE OF CORNELIUS COOT
I'M USUALLY GLAD TO COME HOME AFTER AN EXHAUSTING WOODCHUCK CAMP!
BUT NOT THIS TIME! I COULD HAVE STAYED ANOTHER TWO WEEKS!
Donald Duck
ALL THANKS TO THE CAMP'S FOCUS– THE JUNIOR WOODCHUCK GUIDEBOOK!
D 2003-187
I HAVE TO HAND IT TO OUR L.I.T.E.R.A.R.Y. L.I.O.N.* FOR THE IDEA!
HE FELT WE NEEDED TO IMMERSE OURSELVES IN UNDERSTANDING THE GUIDEBOOK'S RATHER "ORIGINAL" INDEXING SYSTEM!
Donald Duck
*LAURELED INVESTIGATOR OF TOTAL ENIGMAS, RIDDLES, AND RIP-ROARING YARNS, LIBRARIAN IN ORDINARY NOMENCLATURE.
BUT NOW WE KNOW THAT TO FIND THE TRUTH BEHIND THE LEGEND OF KING ARTHUR, WE HAVE TO LOOK UNDER "FURNITURE-TABLES-ROUND!"
MAN, KNOWLEDGE SURE IS FUN!
I CAN'T WAIT TO LOOK UP MORE PERPLEXING QUESTIONS!
GASP! I CAN'T WAIT...
...TO FIND OUT WHY UNCA DONALD HAS TURNED OUR LIVING ROOM INTO SOMETHING RESEMBLING MOONBASE ALPHA!

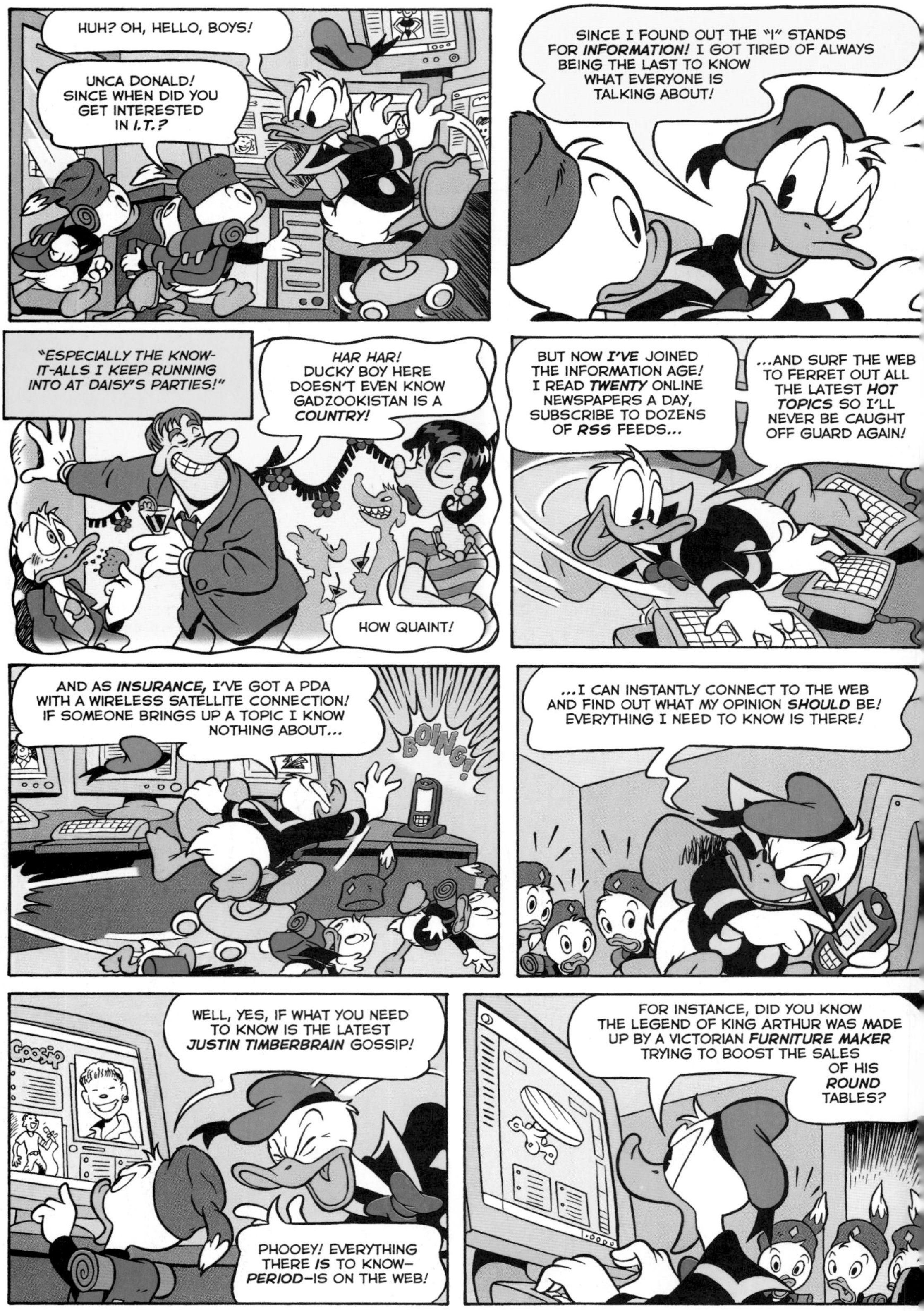

UNCA DONALD! SINCE WHEN DID YOU GET INTERESTED IN *I.T.?*
HUH? OH, HELLO, BOYS!
SINCE I FOUND OUT THE "I" STANDS FOR ***INFORMATION!*** I GOT TIRED OF ALWAYS BEING THE LAST TO KNOW WHAT EVERYONE IS TALKING ABOUT!
"ESPECIALLY THE KNOW-IT-ALLS I KEEP RUNNING INTO AT DAISY'S PARTIES!"
HAR HAR! DUCKY BOY HERE DOESN'T EVEN KNOW GADZOOKISTAN IS A ***COUNTRY!***
HOW QUAINT!
BUT NOW ***I'VE*** JOINED THE INFORMATION AGE! I READ ***TWENTY*** ONLINE NEWSPAPERS A DAY, SUBSCRIBE TO DOZENS OF ***RSS*** FEEDS...
...AND SURF THE WEB TO FERRET OUT ALL THE LATEST ***HOT TOPICS*** SO I'LL NEVER BE CAUGHT OFF GUARD AGAIN!
AND AS ***INSURANCE,*** I'VE GOT A PDA WITH A WIRELESS SATELLITE CONNECTION! IF SOMEONE BRINGS UP A TOPIC I KNOW NOTHING ABOUT...
BOING!
...I CAN INSTANTLY CONNECT TO THE WEB AND FIND OUT WHAT MY OPINION ***SHOULD*** BE! EVERYTHING I NEED TO KNOW IS THERE!
GOSSIP
WELL, YES, IF WHAT YOU NEED TO KNOW IS THE LATEST ***JUSTIN TIMBERBRAIN*** GOSSIP!
PHOOEY! EVERYTHING THERE ***IS*** TO KNOW—***PERIOD***—IS ON THE WEB!
FOR INSTANCE, DID YOU KNOW THE LEGEND OF KING ARTHUR WAS MADE UP BY A VICTORIAN ***FURNITURE MAKER*** TRYING TO BOOST THE SALES OF HIS ***ROUND*** TABLES?

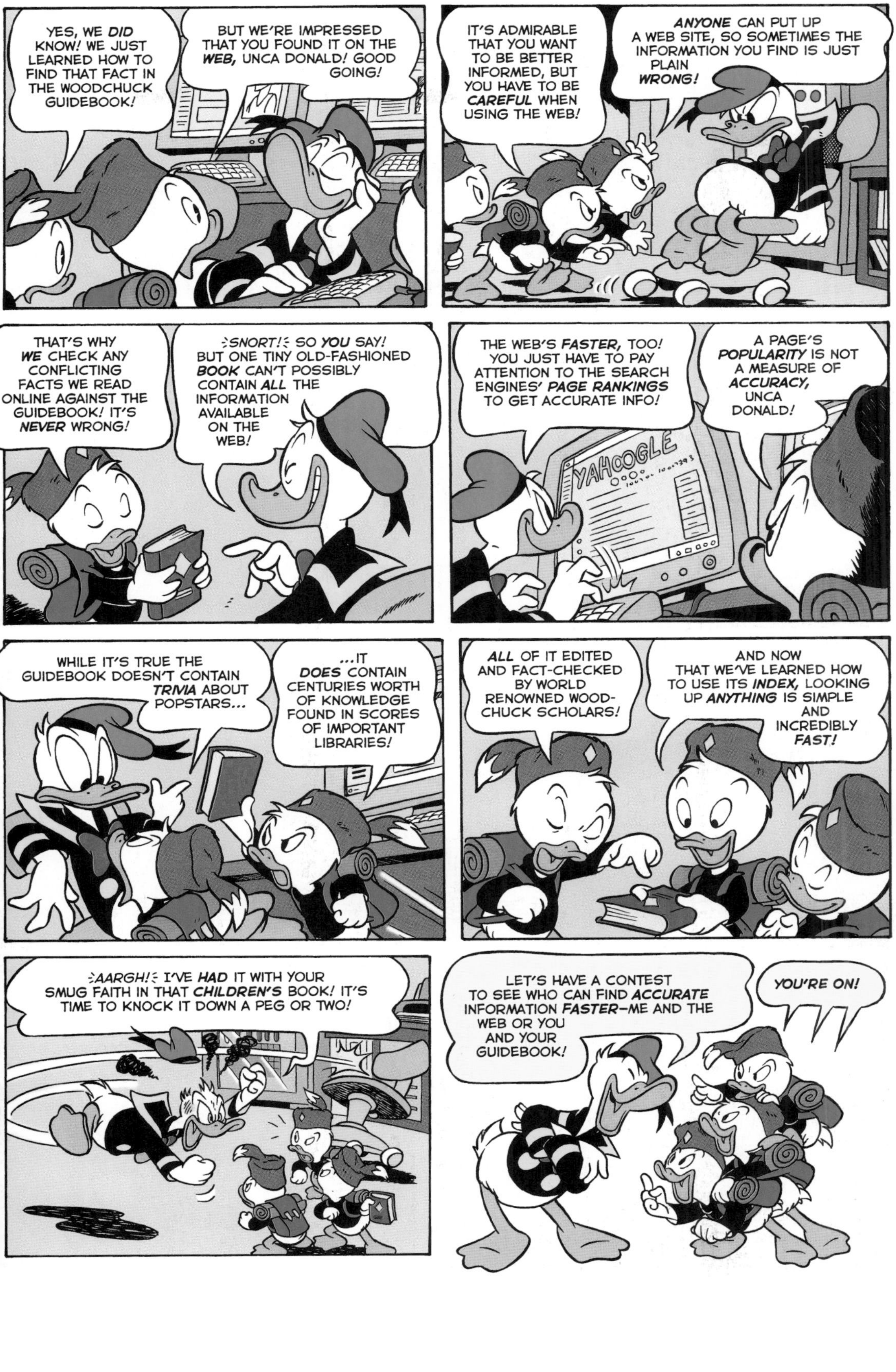
YES, WE DID KNOW! WE JUST LEARNED HOW TO FIND THAT FACT IN THE WOODCHUCK GUIDEBOOK!
BUT WE'RE IMPRESSED THAT YOU FOUND IT ON THE WEB, UNCA DONALD! GOOD GOING!
IT'S ADMIRABLE THAT YOU WANT TO BE BETTER INFORMED, BUT YOU HAVE TO BE CAREFUL WHEN USING THE WEB!
ANYONE CAN PUT UP A WEB SITE, SO SOMETIMES THE INFORMATION YOU FIND IS JUST PLAIN WRONG!
THAT'S WHY WE CHECK ANY CONFLICTING FACTS WE READ ONLINE AGAINST THE GUIDEBOOK! IT'S NEVER WRONG!
SNORT! SO YOU SAY! BUT ONE TINY OLD-FASHIONED BOOK CAN'T POSSIBLY CONTAIN ALL THE INFORMATION AVAILABLE ON THE WEB!
THE WEB'S FASTER, TOO! YOU JUST HAVE TO PAY ATTENTION TO THE SEARCH ENGINES' PAGE RANKINGS TO GET ACCURATE INFO!
YAHOOGLE
A PAGE'S POPULARITY IS NOT A MEASURE OF ACCURACY, UNCA DONALD!
WHILE IT'S TRUE THE GUIDEBOOK DOESN'T CONTAIN TRIVIA ABOUT POPSTARS...
...IT DOES CONTAIN CENTURIES WORTH OF KNOWLEDGE FOUND IN SCORES OF IMPORTANT LIBRARIES!
ALL OF IT EDITED AND FACT-CHECKED BY WORLD RENOWNED WOOD-CHUCK SCHOLARS!
AND NOW THAT WE'VE LEARNED HOW TO USE ITS INDEX, LOOKING UP ANYTHING IS SIMPLE AND INCREDIBLY FAST!
AARGH! I'VE HAD IT WITH YOUR SMUG FAITH IN THAT CHILDREN'S BOOK! IT'S TIME TO KNOCK IT DOWN A PEG OR TWO!
LET'S HAVE A CONTEST TO SEE WHO CAN FIND ACCURATE INFORMATION FASTER—ME AND THE WEB OR YOU AND YOUR GUIDEBOOK!
YOU'RE ON!

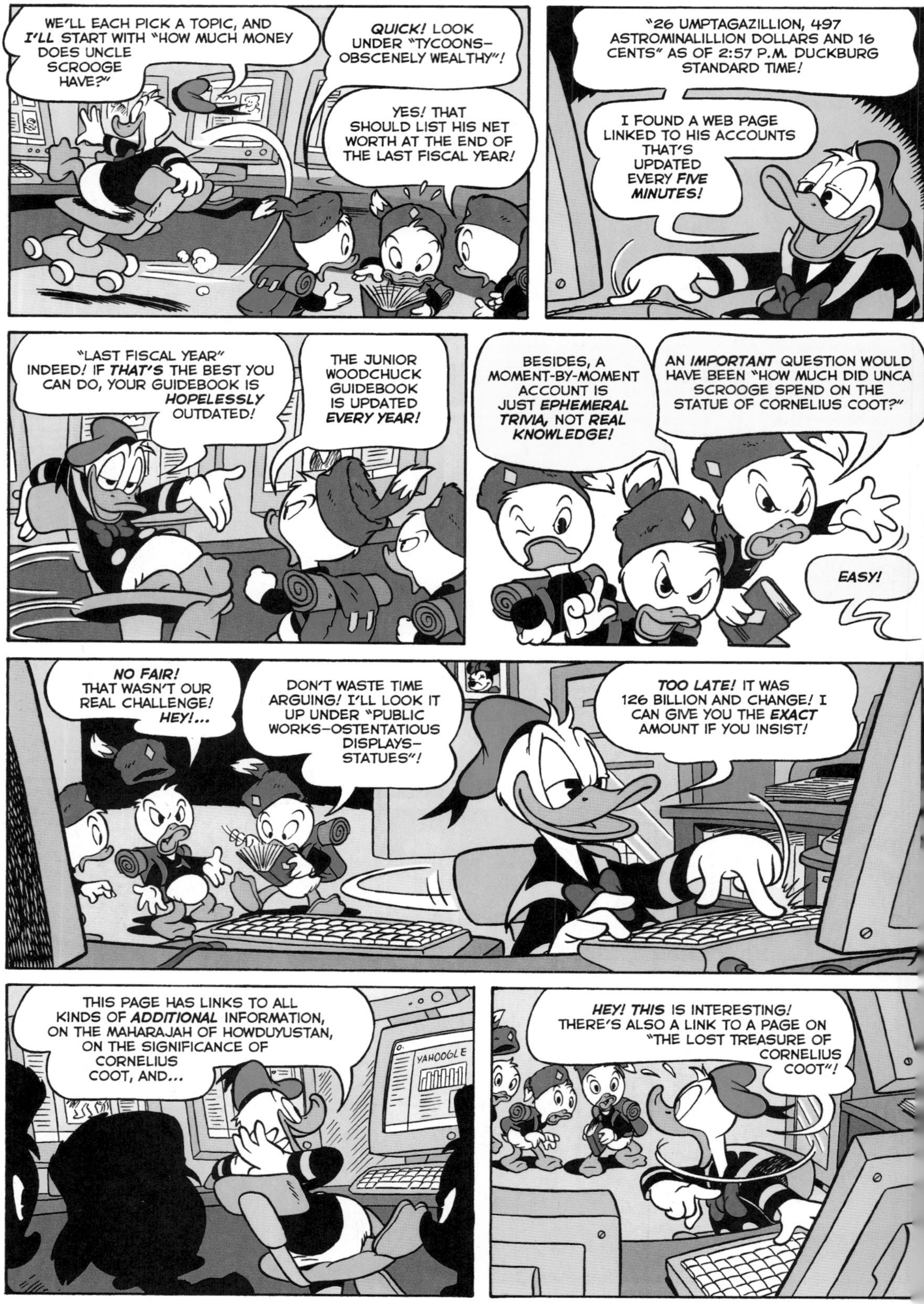
WE'LL EACH PICK A TOPIC, AND I'LL START WITH "HOW MUCH MONEY DOES UNCLE SCROOGE HAVE?"
QUICK! LOOK UNDER "TYCOONS– OBSCENELY WEALTHY"!
YES! THAT SHOULD LIST HIS NET WORTH AT THE END OF THE LAST FISCAL YEAR!
"26 UMPTAGAZILLION, 497 ASTROMINALILLION DOLLARS AND 16 CENTS" AS OF 2:57 P.M. DUCKBURG STANDARD TIME!
I FOUND A WEB PAGE LINKED TO HIS ACCOUNTS THAT'S UPDATED EVERY FIVE MINUTES!
"LAST FISCAL YEAR" INDEED! IF THAT'S THE BEST YOU CAN DO, YOUR GUIDEBOOK IS HOPELESSLY OUTDATED!
THE JUNIOR WOODCHUCK GUIDEBOOK IS UPDATED EVERY YEAR!
BESIDES, A MOMENT-BY-MOMENT ACCOUNT IS JUST EPHEMERAL TRIVIA, NOT REAL KNOWLEDGE!
AN IMPORTANT QUESTION WOULD HAVE BEEN "HOW MUCH DID UNCA SCROOGE SPEND ON THE STATUE OF CORNELIUS COOT?"
EASY!
NO FAIR! THAT WASN'T OUR REAL CHALLENGE! HEY!...
DON'T WASTE TIME ARGUING! I'LL LOOK IT UP UNDER "PUBLIC WORKS–OSTENTATIOUS DISPLAYS– STATUES"!
TOO LATE! IT WAS 126 BILLION AND CHANGE! I CAN GIVE YOU THE EXACT AMOUNT IF YOU INSIST!
THIS PAGE HAS LINKS TO ALL KINDS OF ADDITIONAL INFORMATION, ON THE MAHARAJAH OF HOWDUYUSTAN, ON THE SIGNIFICANCE OF CORNELIUS COOT, AND...
YAHOOGLE
HEY! THIS IS INTERESTING! THERE'S ALSO A LINK TO A PAGE ON "THE LOST TREASURE OF CORNELIUS COOT"!

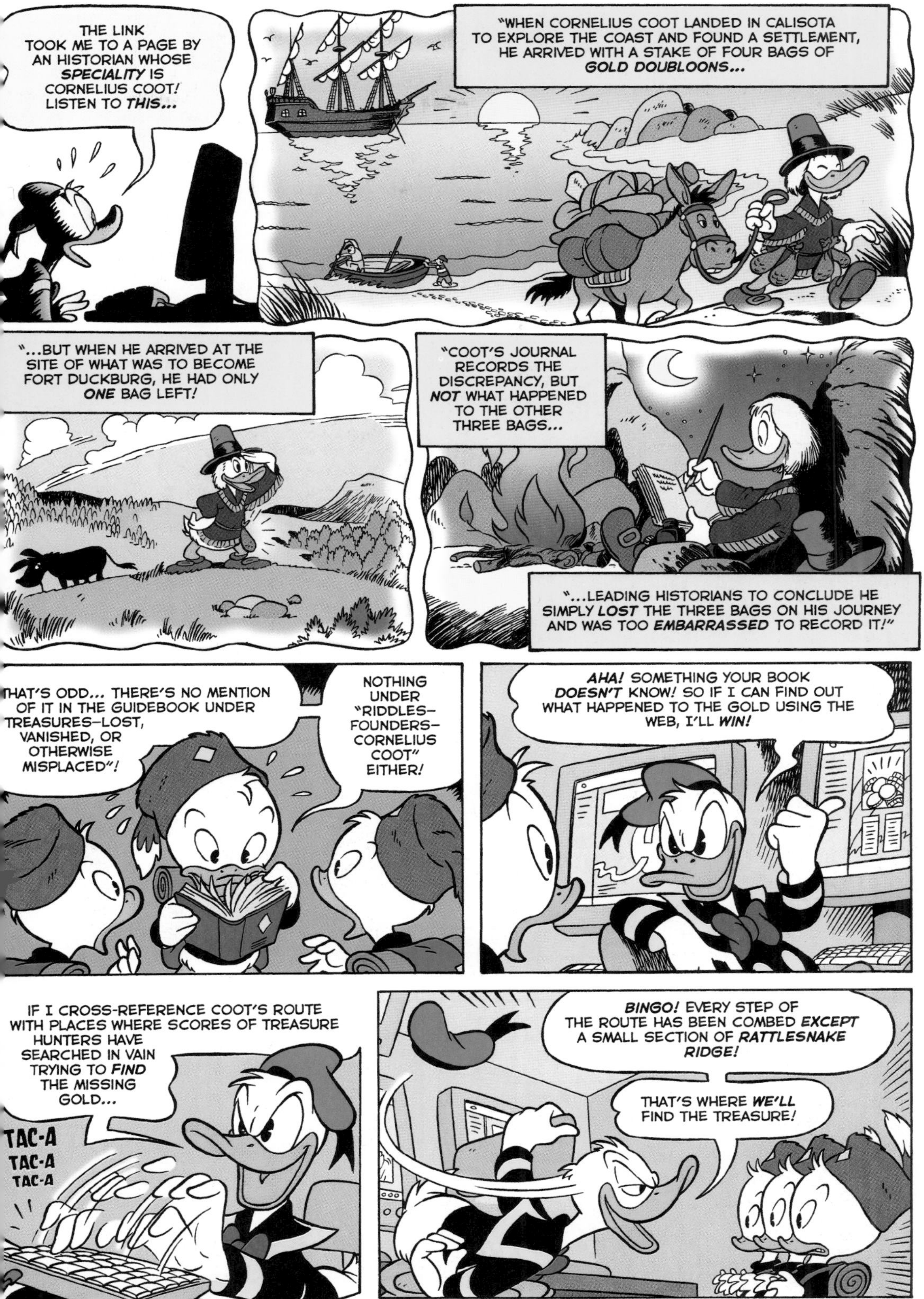
THE LINK TOOK ME TO A PAGE BY AN HISTORIAN WHOSE SPECIALITY IS CORNELIUS COOT! LISTEN TO THIS...
"WHEN CORNELIUS COOT LANDED IN CALISOTA TO EXPLORE THE COAST AND FOUND A SETTLEMENT, HE ARRIVED WITH A STAKE OF FOUR BAGS OF GOLD DOUBLOONS...
"...BUT WHEN HE ARRIVED AT THE SITE OF WHAT WAS TO BECOME FORT DUCKBURG, HE HAD ONLY ONE BAG LEFT!
"COOT'S JOURNAL RECORDS THE DISCREPANCY, BUT NOT WHAT HAPPENED TO THE OTHER THREE BAGS...
"...LEADING HISTORIANS TO CONCLUDE HE SIMPLY LOST THE THREE BAGS ON HIS JOURNEY AND WAS TOO EMBARRASSED TO RECORD IT!"
THAT'S ODD... THERE'S NO MENTION OF IT IN THE GUIDEBOOK UNDER TREASURES–LOST, VANISHED, OR OTHERWISE MISPLACED"!
NOTHING UNDER "RIDDLES–FOUNDERS–CORNELIUS COOT" EITHER!
AHA! SOMETHING YOUR BOOK DOESN'T KNOW! SO IF I CAN FIND OUT WHAT HAPPENED TO THE GOLD USING THE WEB, I'LL WIN!
IF I CROSS-REFERENCE COOT'S ROUTE WITH PLACES WHERE SCORES OF TREASURE HUNTERS HAVE SEARCHED IN VAIN TRYING TO FIND THE MISSING GOLD...
TAC-A
TAC-A
TAC-A
BINGO! EVERY STEP OF THE ROUTE HAS BEEN COMBED EXCEPT A SMALL SECTION OF RATTLESNAKE RIDGE!
THAT'S WHERE WE'LL FIND THE TREASURE!

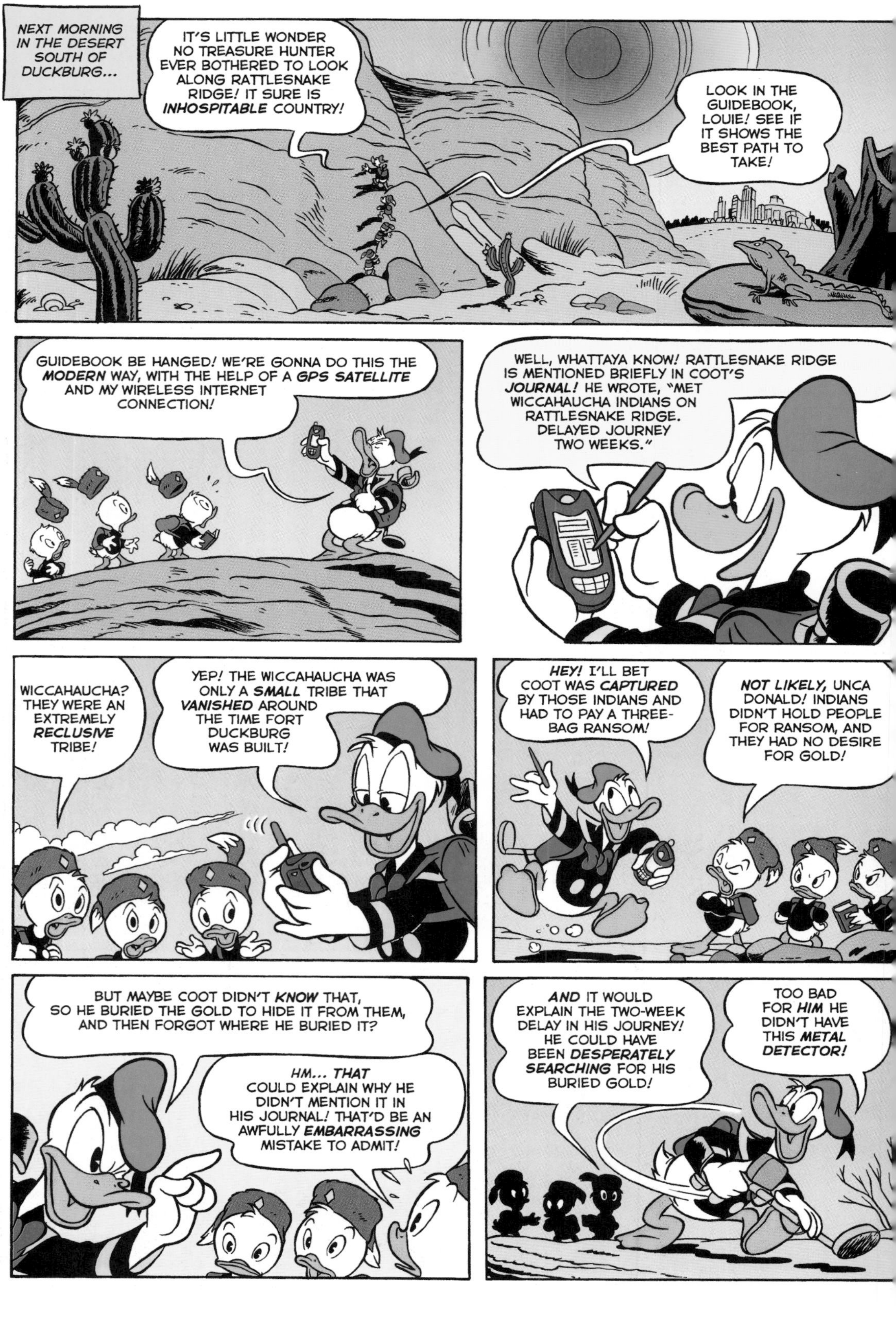
NEXT MORNING IN THE DESERT SOUTH OF DUCKBURG...
IT'S LITTLE WONDER NO TREASURE HUNTER EVER BOTHERED TO LOOK ALONG RATTLESNAKE RIDGE! IT SURE IS INHOSPITABLE COUNTRY!
LOOK IN THE GUIDEBOOK, LOUIE! SEE IF IT SHOWS THE BEST PATH TO TAKE!
GUIDEBOOK BE HANGED! WE'RE GONNA DO THIS THE MODERN WAY, WITH THE HELP OF A GPS SATELLITE AND MY WIRELESS INTERNET CONNECTION!
WELL, WHATTAYA KNOW! RATTLESNAKE RIDGE IS MENTIONED BRIEFLY IN COOT'S JOURNAL! HE WROTE, "MET WICCAHAUCHA INDIANS ON RATTLESNAKE RIDGE. DELAYED JOURNEY TWO WEEKS."
WICCAHAUCHA? THEY WERE AN EXTREMELY RECLUSIVE TRIBE!
YEP! THE WICCAHAUCHA WAS ONLY A SMALL TRIBE THAT VANISHED AROUND THE TIME FORT DUCKBURG WAS BUILT!
HEY! I'LL BET COOT WAS CAPTURED BY THOSE INDIANS AND HAD TO PAY A THREE-BAG RANSOM!
NOT LIKELY, UNCA DONALD! INDIANS DIDN'T HOLD PEOPLE FOR RANSOM, AND THEY HAD NO DESIRE FOR GOLD!
BUT MAYBE COOT DIDN'T KNOW THAT, SO HE BURIED THE GOLD TO HIDE IT FROM THEM, AND THEN FORGOT WHERE HE BURIED IT?
HM... THAT COULD EXPLAIN WHY HE DIDN'T MENTION IT IN HIS JOURNAL! THAT'D BE AN AWFULLY EMBARRASSING MISTAKE TO ADMIT!
AND IT WOULD EXPLAIN THE TWO-WEEK DELAY IN HIS JOURNEY! HE COULD HAVE BEEN DESPERATELY SEARCHING FOR HIS BURIED GOLD!
TOO BAD FOR HIM HE DIDN'T HAVE THIS METAL DETECTOR!

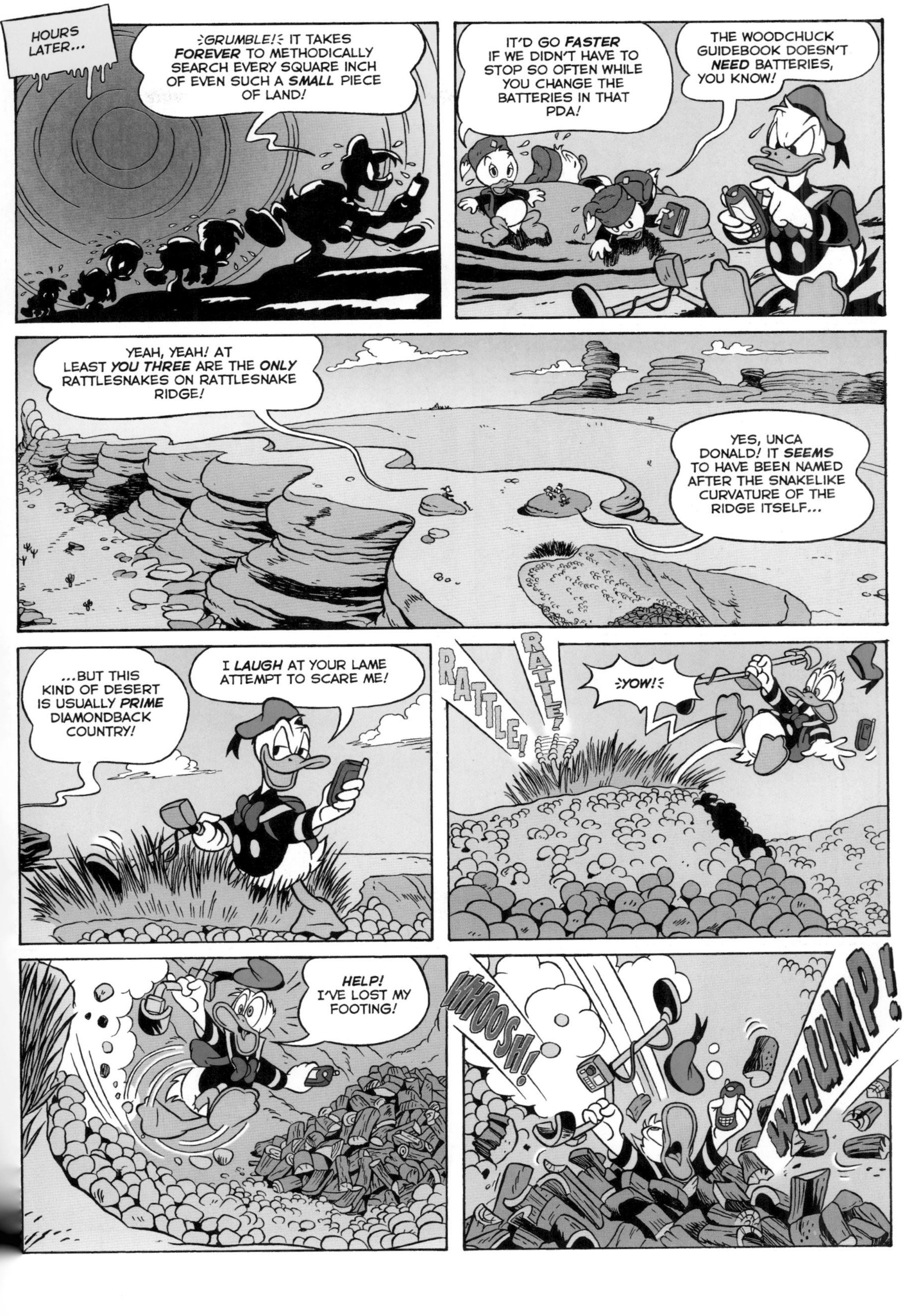
HOURS LATER...
GRUMBLE! IT TAKES FOREVER TO METHODICALLY SEARCH EVERY SQUARE INCH OF EVEN SUCH A SMALL PIECE OF LAND!
IT'D GO FASTER IF WE DIDN'T HAVE TO STOP SO OFTEN WHILE YOU CHANGE THE BATTERIES IN THAT PDA!
THE WOODCHUCK GUIDEBOOK DOESN'T NEED BATTERIES, YOU KNOW!
YEAH, YEAH! AT LEAST YOU THREE ARE THE ONLY RATTLESNAKES ON RATTLESNAKE RIDGE!
YES, UNCA DONALD! IT SEEMS TO HAVE BEEN NAMED AFTER THE SNAKELIKE CURVATURE OF THE RIDGE ITSELF...
...BUT THIS KIND OF DESERT IS USUALLY PRIME DIAMONDBACK COUNTRY!
I LAUGH AT YOUR LAME ATTEMPT TO SCARE ME!
RATTLE!
RATTLE!
YOW!
HELP! I'VE LOST MY FOOTING!
WHOOSH!
WHUMP!

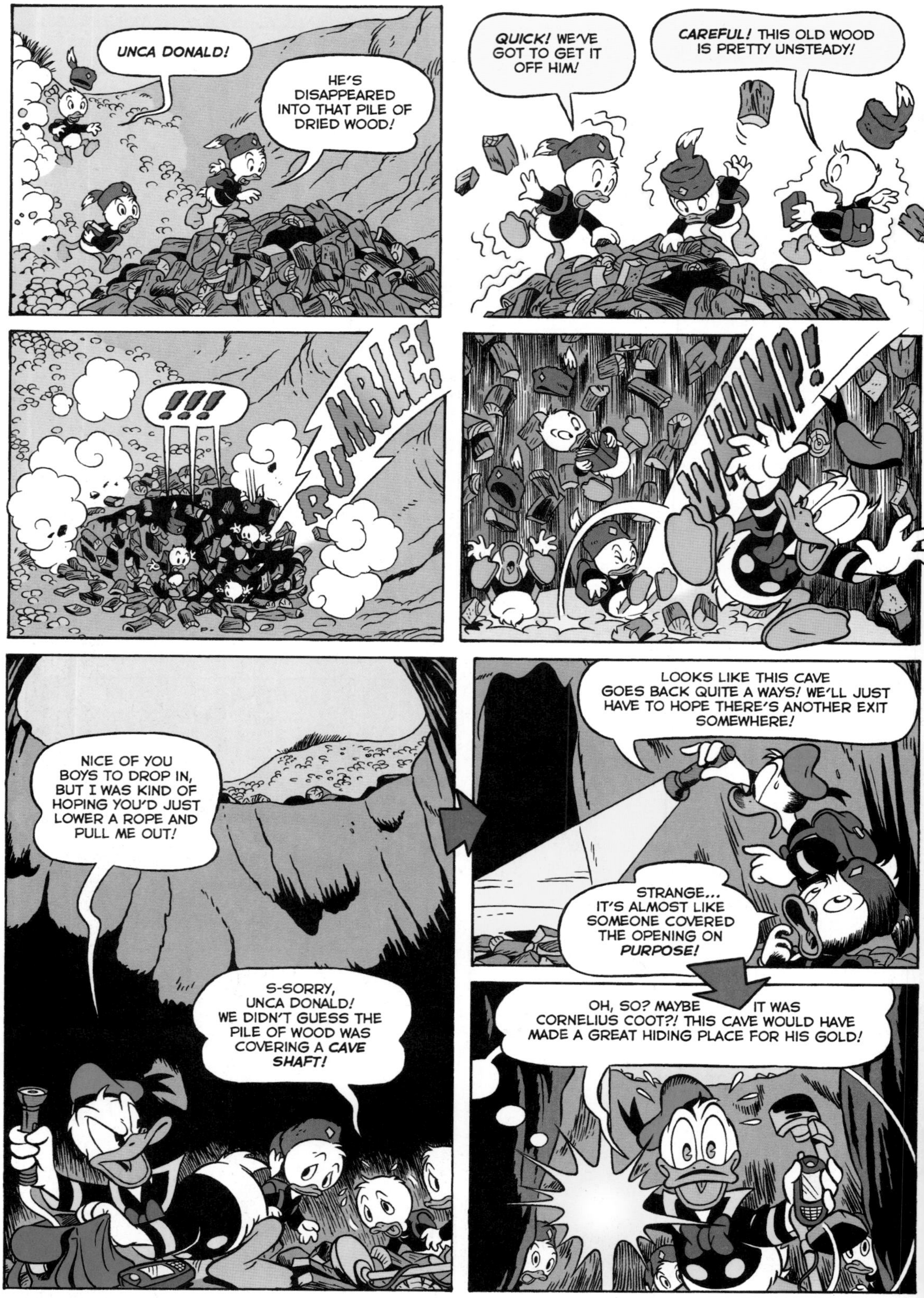
UNCA DONALD!
HE'S DISAPPEARED INTO THAT PILE OF DRIED WOOD!
QUICK! WE'VE GOT TO GET IT OFF HIM!
CAREFUL! THIS OLD WOOD IS PRETTY UNSTEADY!
!!!
RUMBLE!
WHUMP!
NICE OF YOU BOYS TO DROP IN, BUT I WAS KIND OF HOPING YOU'D JUST LOWER A ROPE AND PULL ME OUT!
S-SORRY, UNCA DONALD! WE DIDN'T GUESS THE PILE OF WOOD WAS COVERING A CAVE SHAFT!
LOOKS LIKE THIS CAVE GOES BACK QUITE A WAYS! WE'LL JUST HAVE TO HOPE THERE'S ANOTHER EXIT SOMEWHERE!
STRANGE... IT'S ALMOST LIKE SOMEONE COVERED THE OPENING ON PURPOSE!
OH, SO? MAYBE IT WAS CORNELIUS COOT?! THIS CAVE WOULD HAVE MADE A GREAT HIDING PLACE FOR HIS GOLD!

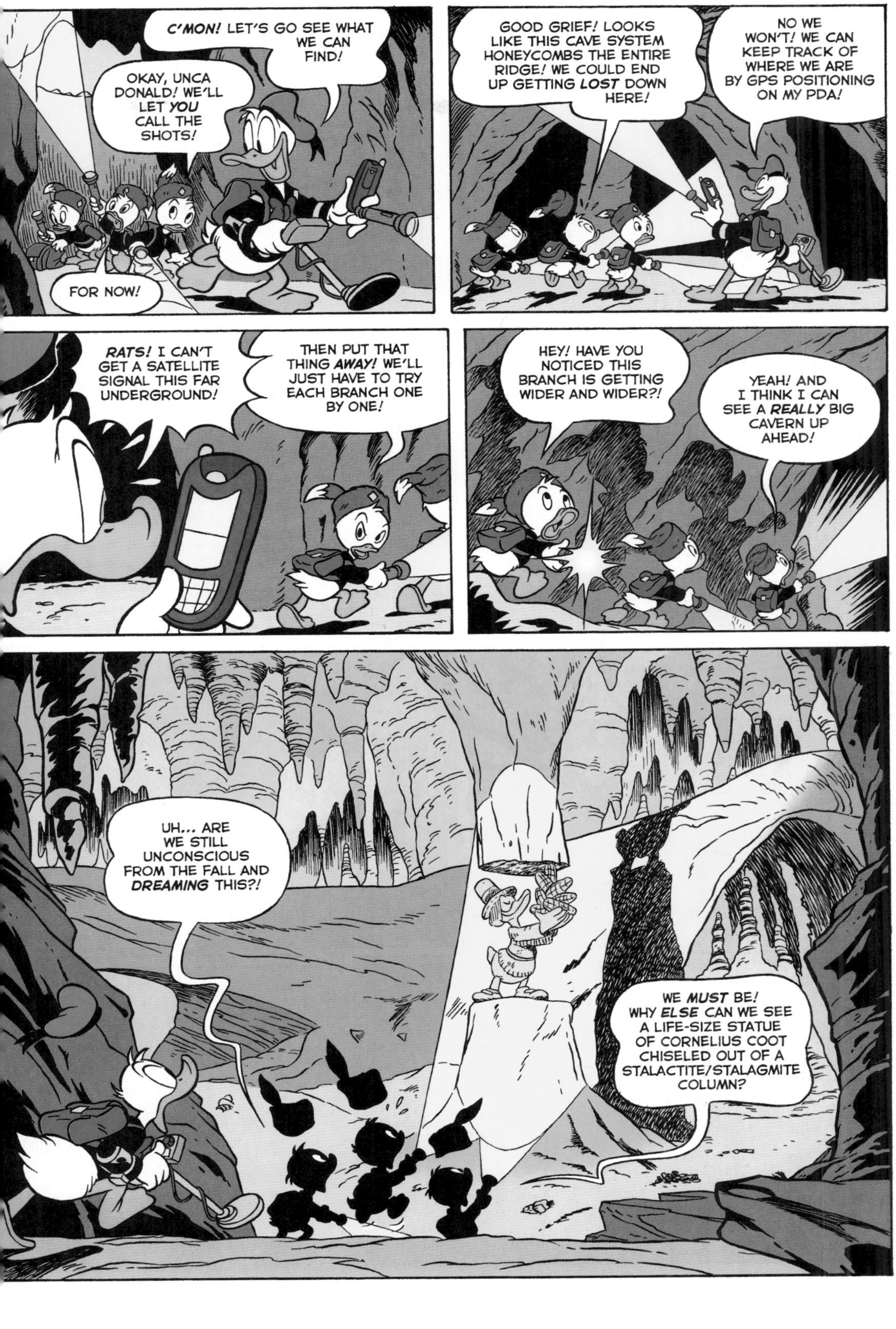
C'MON! LET'S GO SEE WHAT WE CAN FIND!
OKAY, UNCA DONALD! WE'LL LET YOU CALL THE SHOTS!
FOR NOW!
GOOD GRIEF! LOOKS LIKE THIS CAVE SYSTEM HONEYCOMBS THE ENTIRE RIDGE! WE COULD END UP GETTING LOST DOWN HERE!
NO WE WON'T! WE CAN KEEP TRACK OF WHERE WE ARE BY GPS POSITIONING ON MY PDA!
RATS! I CAN'T GET A SATELLITE SIGNAL THIS FAR UNDERGROUND!
THEN PUT THAT THING AWAY! WE'LL JUST HAVE TO TRY EACH BRANCH ONE BY ONE!
HEY! HAVE YOU NOTICED THIS BRANCH IS GETTING WIDER AND WIDER?!
YEAH! AND I THINK I CAN SEE A REALLY BIG CAVERN UP AHEAD!
UH... ARE WE STILL UNCONSCIOUS FROM THE FALL AND DREAMING THIS?!
WE MUST BE! WHY ELSE CAN WE SEE A LIFE-SIZE STATUE OF CORNELIUS COOT CHISELED OUT OF A STALACTITE/STALAGMITE COLUMN?

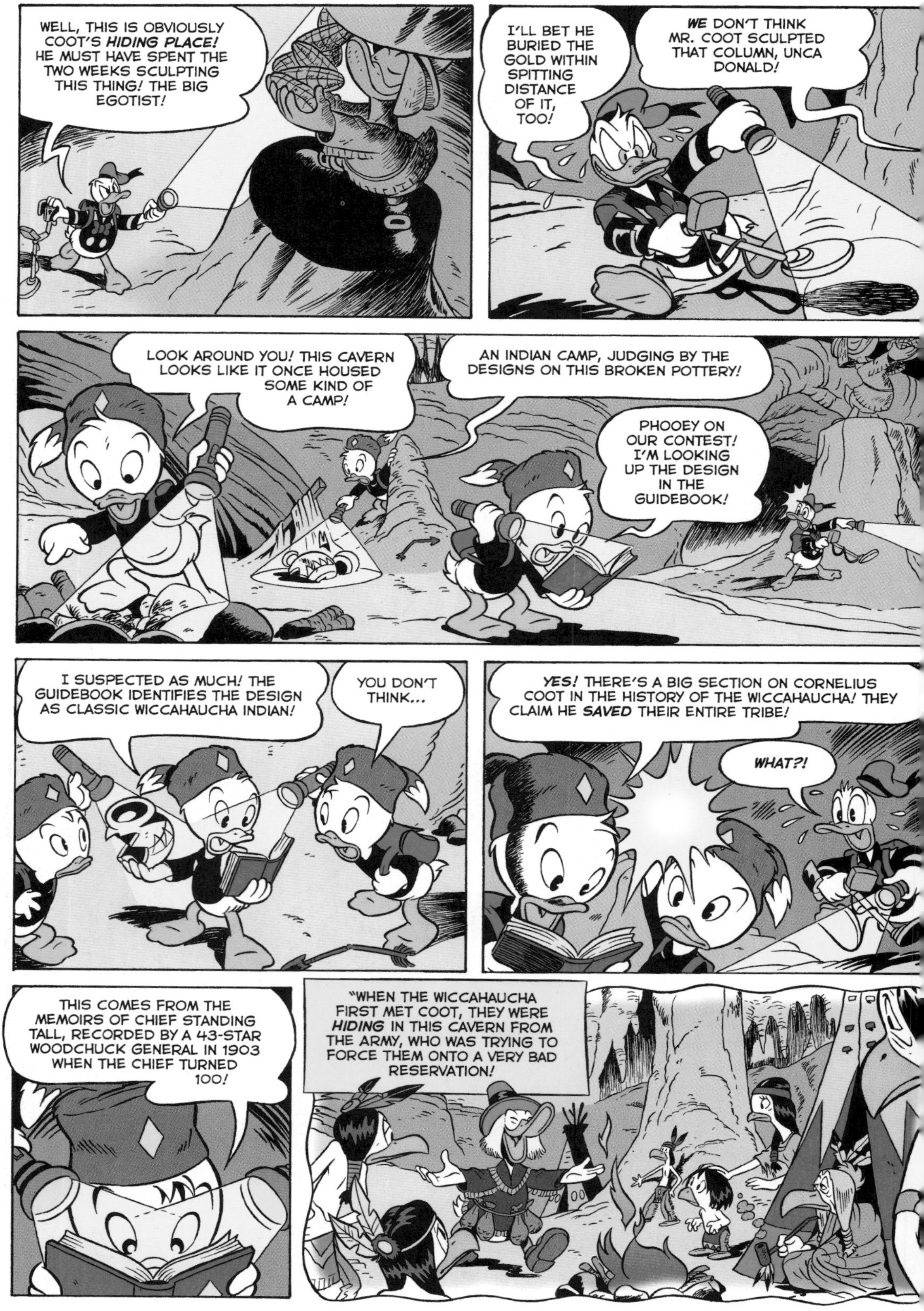
WELL, THIS IS OBVIOUSLY COOT'S HIDING PLACE! HE MUST HAVE SPENT THE TWO WEEKS SCULPTING THIS THING! THE BIG EGOTIST!
I'LL BET HE BURIED THE GOLD WITHIN SPITTING DISTANCE OF IT, TOO!
WE DON'T THINK MR. COOT SCULPTED THAT COLUMN, UNCA DONALD!
LOOK AROUND YOU! THIS CAVERN LOOKS LIKE IT ONCE HOUSED SOME KIND OF A CAMP!
AN INDIAN CAMP, JUDGING BY THE DESIGNS ON THIS BROKEN POTTERY!
PHOOEY ON OUR CONTEST! I'M LOOKING UP THE DESIGN IN THE GUIDEBOOK!
I SUSPECTED AS MUCH! THE GUIDEBOOK IDENTIFIES THE DESIGN AS CLASSIC WICCAHAUCHA INDIAN!
YOU DON'T THINK...
YES! THERE'S A BIG SECTION ON CORNELIUS COOT IN THE HISTORY OF THE WICCAHAUCHA! THEY CLAIM HE SAVED THEIR ENTIRE TRIBE!
WHAT?!
THIS COMES FROM THE MEMOIRS OF CHIEF STANDING TALL, RECORDED BY A 43-STAR WOODCHUCK GENERAL IN 1903 WHEN THE CHIEF TURNED 100!
"WHEN THE WICCAHAUCHA FIRST MET COOT, THEY WERE HIDING IN THIS CAVERN FROM THE ARMY, WHO WAS TRYING TO FORCE THEM ONTO A VERY BAD RESERVATION!

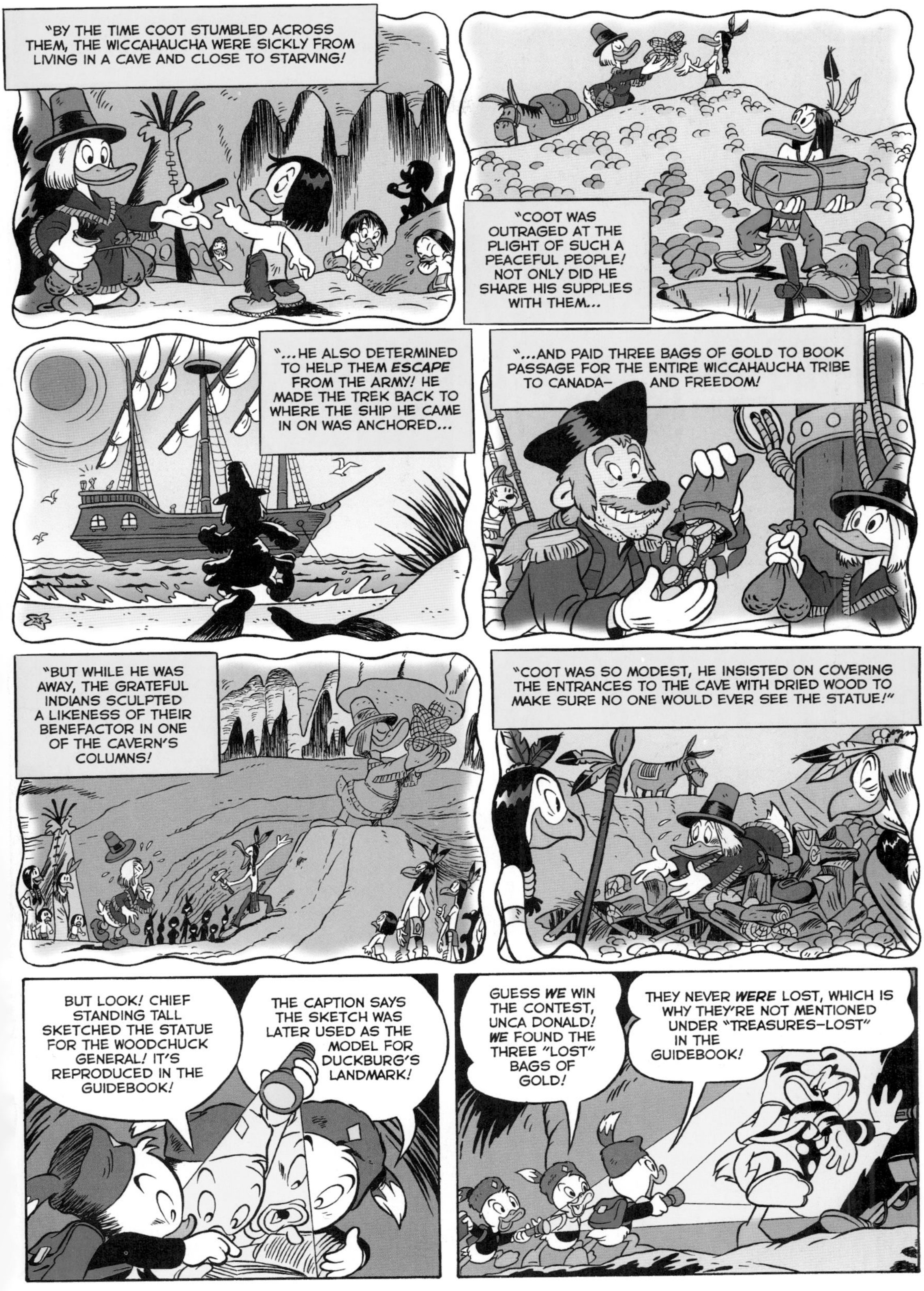
"BY THE TIME COOT STUMBLED ACROSS THEM, THE WICCAHAUCHA WERE SICKLY FROM LIVING IN A CAVE AND CLOSE TO STARVING!
"COOT WAS OUTRAGED AT THE PLIGHT OF SUCH A PEACEFUL PEOPLE! NOT ONLY DID HE SHARE HIS SUPPLIES WITH THEM...
"...HE ALSO DETERMINED TO HELP THEM ESCAPE FROM THE ARMY! HE MADE THE TREK BACK TO WHERE THE SHIP HE CAME IN ON WAS ANCHORED...
"...AND PAID THREE BAGS OF GOLD TO BOOK PASSAGE FOR THE ENTIRE WICCAHAUCHA TRIBE TO CANADA— AND FREEDOM!
"BUT WHILE HE WAS AWAY, THE GRATEFUL INDIANS SCULPTED A LIKENESS OF THEIR BENEFACTOR IN ONE OF THE CAVERN'S COLUMNS!
"COOT WAS SO MODEST, HE INSISTED ON COVERING THE ENTRANCES TO THE CAVE WITH DRIED WOOD TO MAKE SURE NO ONE WOULD EVER SEE THE STATUE!"
BUT LOOK! CHIEF STANDING TALL SKETCHED THE STATUE FOR THE WOODCHUCK GENERAL! IT'S REPRODUCED IN THE GUIDEBOOK!
THE CAPTION SAYS THE SKETCH WAS LATER USED AS THE MODEL FOR DUCKBURG'S LANDMARK!
GUESS WE WIN THE CONTEST, UNCA DONALD! WE FOUND THE THREE "LOST" BAGS OF GOLD!
THEY NEVER WERE LOST, WHICH IS WHY THEY'RE NOT MENTIONED UNDER "TREASURES–LOST" IN THE GUIDEBOOK!

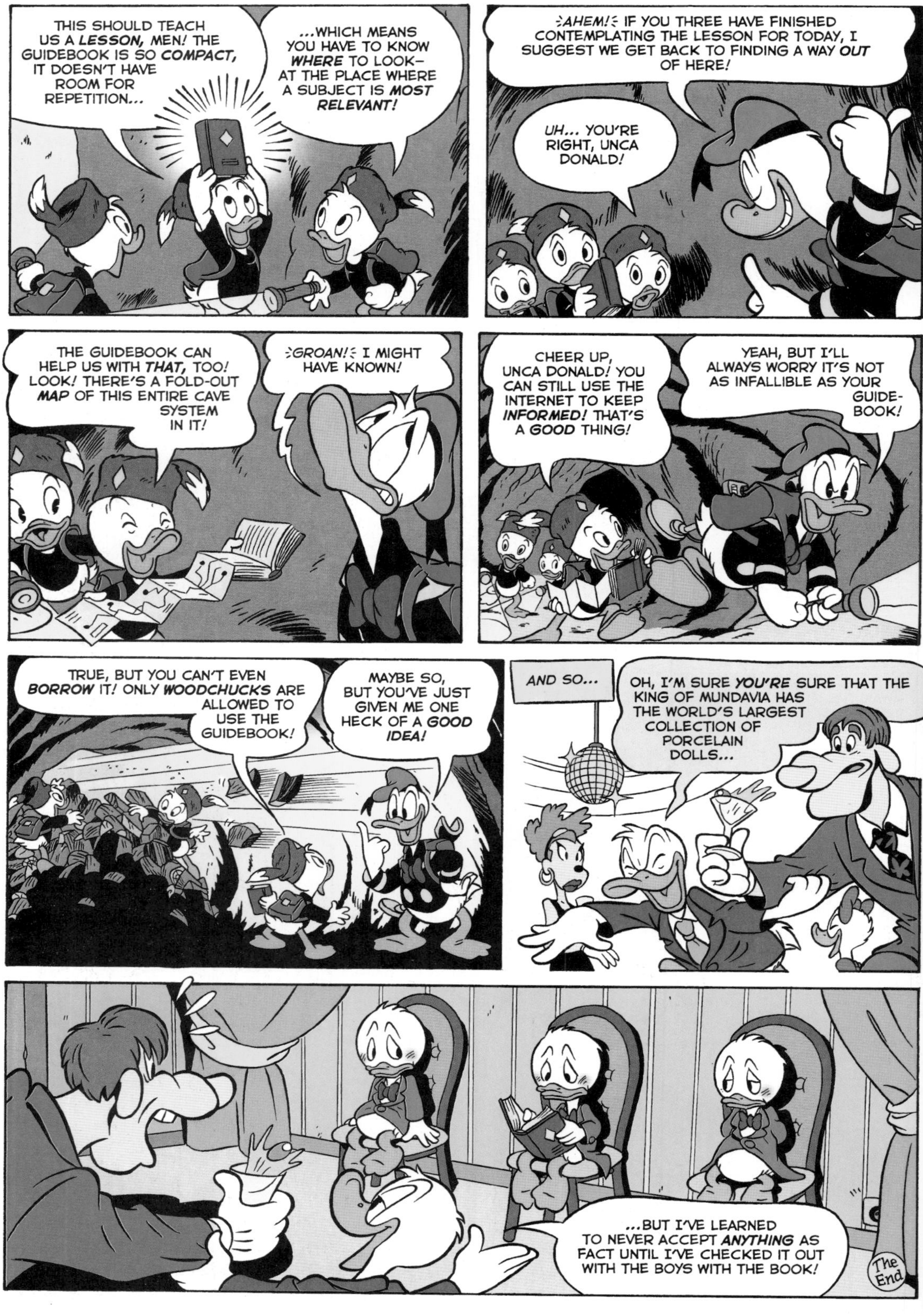
THIS SHOULD TEACH US A LESSON, MEN! THE GUIDEBOOK IS SO COMPACT, IT DOESN'T HAVE ROOM FOR REPETITION...
...WHICH MEANS YOU HAVE TO KNOW WHERE TO LOOK— AT THE PLACE WHERE A SUBJECT IS MOST RELEVANT!
AHEM! IF YOU THREE HAVE FINISHED CONTEMPLATING THE LESSON FOR TODAY, I SUGGEST WE GET BACK TO FINDING A WAY OUT OF HERE!
UH... YOU'RE RIGHT, UNCA DONALD!
THE GUIDEBOOK CAN HELP US WITH THAT, TOO! LOOK! THERE'S A FOLD-OUT MAP OF THIS ENTIRE CAVE SYSTEM IN IT!
GROAN! I MIGHT HAVE KNOWN!
CHEER UP, UNCA DONALD! YOU CAN STILL USE THE INTERNET TO KEEP INFORMED! THAT'S A GOOD THING!
YEAH, BUT I'LL ALWAYS WORRY IT'S NOT AS INFALLIBLE AS YOUR GUIDE-BOOK!
TRUE, BUT YOU CAN'T EVEN BORROW IT! ONLY WOODCHUCKS ARE ALLOWED TO USE THE GUIDEBOOK!
MAYBE SO, BUT YOU'VE JUST GIVEN ME ONE HECK OF A GOOD IDEA!
AND SO...
OH, I'M SURE YOU'RE SURE THAT THE KING OF MUNDAVIA HAS THE WORLD'S LARGEST COLLECTION OF PORCELAIN DOLLS...
...BUT I'VE LEARNED TO NEVER ACCEPT ANYTHING AS FACT UNTIL I'VE CHECKED IT OUT WITH THE BOYS WITH THE BOOK!
The End

Walt Disney's Mickey Mouse in Free Weegie

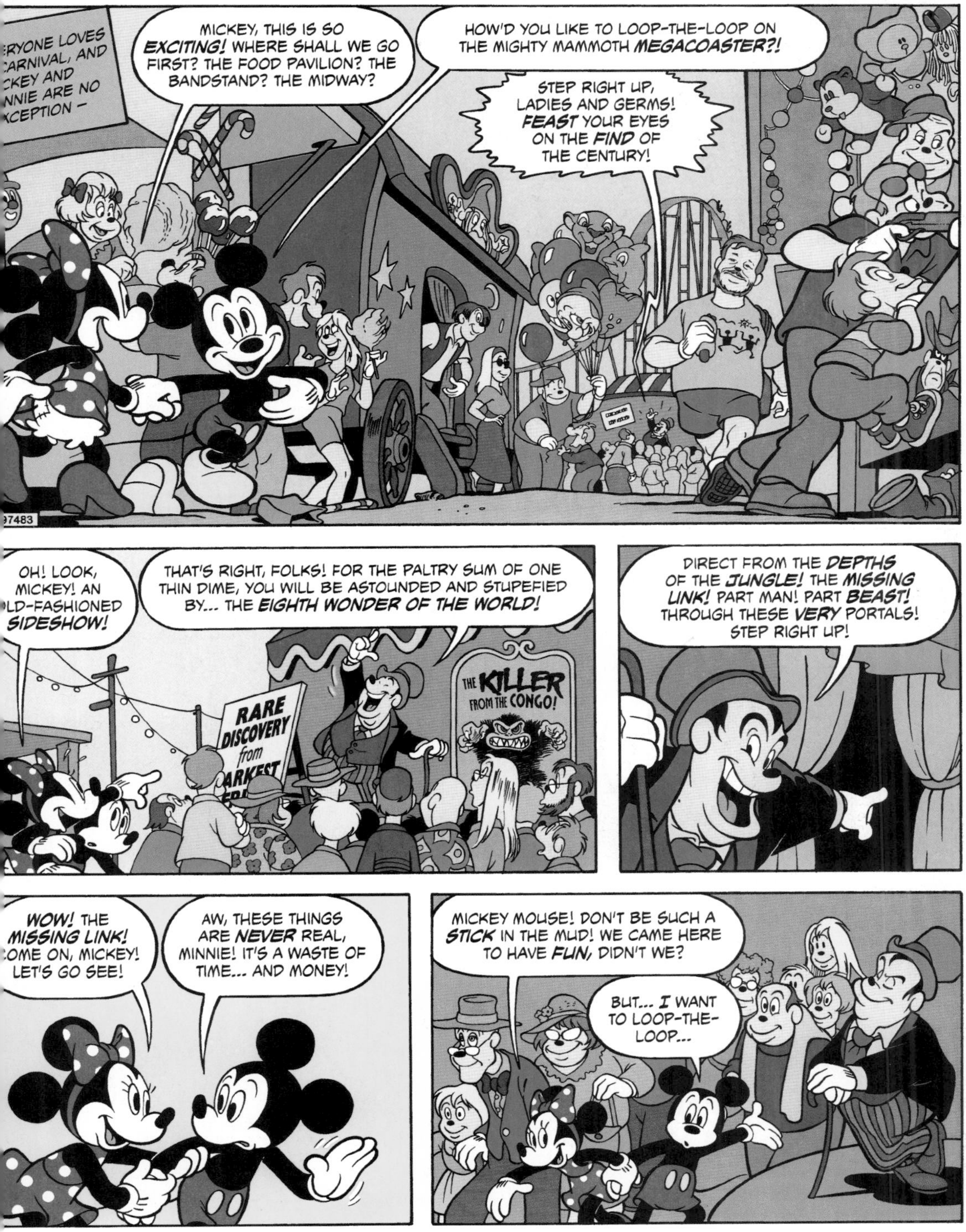

ERYONE LOVES CARNIVAL, AND CKEY AND NNIE ARE NO XCEPTION –
MICKEY, THIS IS SO EXCITING! WHERE SHALL WE GO FIRST? THE FOOD PAVILION? THE BANDSTAND? THE MIDWAY?
HOW'D YOU LIKE TO LOOP-THE-LOOP ON THE MIGHTY MAMMOTH MEGACOASTER?!
STEP RIGHT UP, LADIES AND GERMS! FEAST YOUR EYES ON THE FIND OF THE CENTURY!
97483
OH! LOOK, MICKEY! AN LD-FASHIONED SIDESHOW!
THAT'S RIGHT, FOLKS! FOR THE PALTRY SUM OF ONE THIN DIME, YOU WILL BE ASTOUNDED AND STUPEFIED BY... THE EIGHTH WONDER OF THE WORLD!
RARE DISCOVERY from
THE KILLER FROM THE CONGO!
DIRECT FROM THE DEPTHS OF THE JUNGLE! THE MISSING LINK! PART MAN! PART BEAST! THROUGH THESE VERY PORTALS! STEP RIGHT UP!
WOW! THE MISSING LINK! OME ON, MICKEY! LET'S GO SEE!
AW, THESE THINGS ARE NEVER REAL, MINNIE! IT'S A WASTE OF TIME... AND MONEY!
MICKEY MOUSE! DON'T BE SUCH A STICK IN THE MUD! WE CAME HERE TO HAVE FUN, DIDN'T WE?
BUT... I WANT TO LOOP-THE-LOOP...

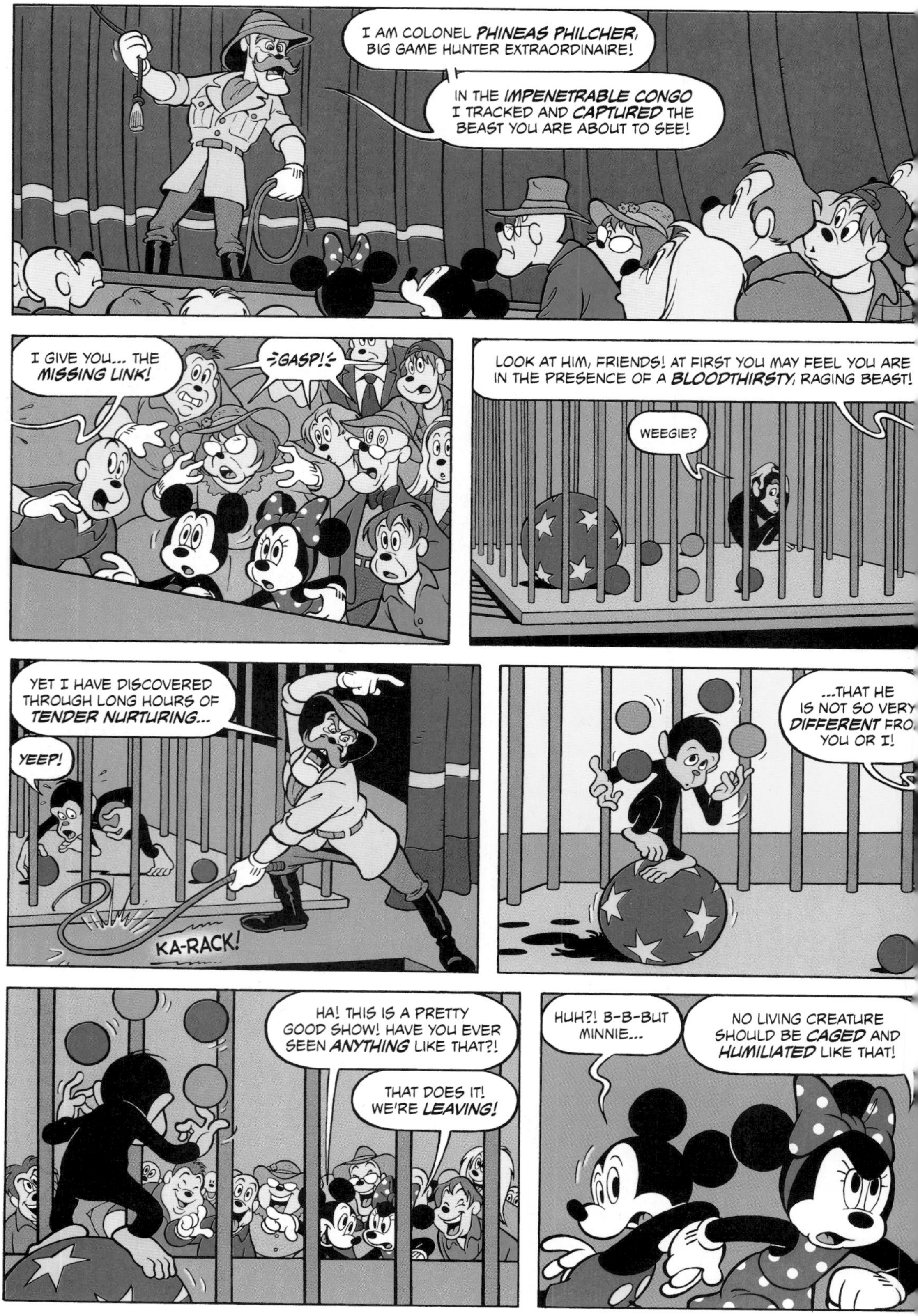
I AM COLONEL PHINEAS PHILCHER, BIG GAME HUNTER EXTRAORDINAIRE!
IN THE IMPENETRABLE CONGO I TRACKED AND CAPTURED THE BEAST YOU ARE ABOUT TO SEE!
I GIVE YOU... THE MISSING LINK!
GASP!
LOOK AT HIM, FRIENDS! AT FIRST YOU MAY FEEL YOU ARE IN THE PRESENCE OF A BLOODTHIRSTY, RAGING BEAST!
WEEGIE?
YET I HAVE DISCOVERED THROUGH LONG HOURS OF TENDER NURTURING...
YEEP!
KA-RACK!
...THAT HE IS NOT SO VERY DIFFERENT FRO YOU OR I!
HA! THIS IS A PRETTY GOOD SHOW! HAVE YOU EVER SEEN ANYTHING LIKE THAT?!
THAT DOES IT! WE'RE LEAVING!
HUH?! B-B-BUT MINNIE...
NO LIVING CREATURE SHOULD BE CAGED AND HUMILIATED LIKE THAT!

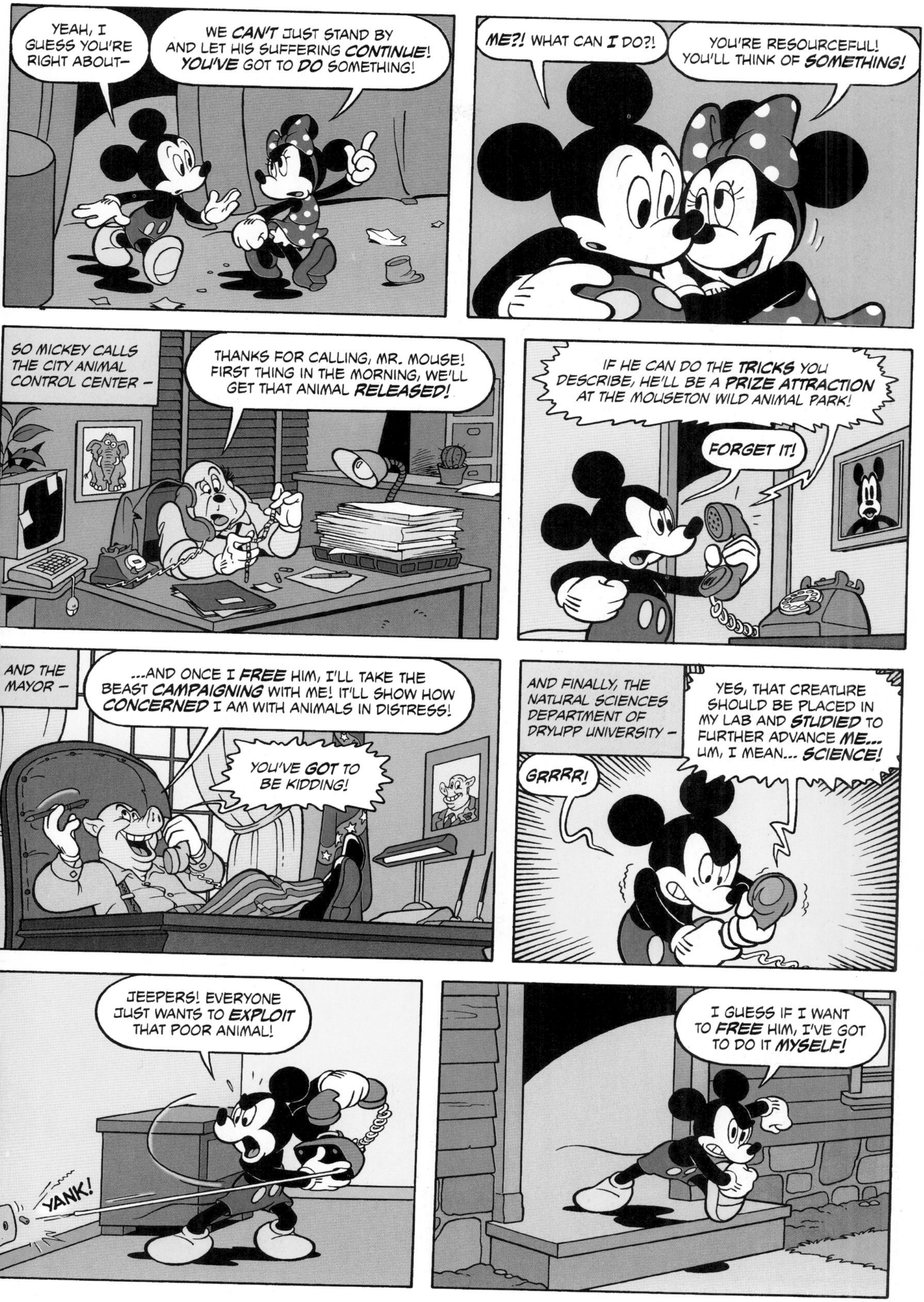
YEAH, I GUESS YOU'RE RIGHT ABOUT–
WE CAN'T JUST STAND BY AND LET HIS SUFFERING CONTINUE! YOU'VE GOT TO DO SOMETHING!
ME?! WHAT CAN I DO?!
YOU'RE RESOURCEFUL! YOU'LL THINK OF SOMETHING!
SO MICKEY CALLS THE CITY ANIMAL CONTROL CENTER –
THANKS FOR CALLING, MR. MOUSE! FIRST THING IN THE MORNING, WE'LL GET THAT ANIMAL RELEASED!
IF HE CAN DO THE TRICKS YOU DESCRIBE, HE'LL BE A PRIZE ATTRACTION AT THE MOUSETON WILD ANIMAL PARK!
FORGET IT!
AND THE MAYOR –
...AND ONCE I FREE HIM, I'LL TAKE THE BEAST CAMPAIGNING WITH ME! IT'LL SHOW HOW CONCERNED I AM WITH ANIMALS IN DISTRESS!
YOU'VE GOT TO BE KIDDING!
AND FINALLY, THE NATURAL SCIENCES DEPARTMENT OF DRYUPP UNIVERSITY –
YES, THAT CREATURE SHOULD BE PLACED IN MY LAB AND STUDIED TO FURTHER ADVANCE ME... UM, I MEAN... SCIENCE!
GRRRR!
JEEPERS! EVERYONE JUST WANTS TO EXPLOIT THAT POOR ANIMAL!
YANK!
I GUESS IF I WANT TO FREE HIM, I'VE GOT TO DO IT MYSELF!

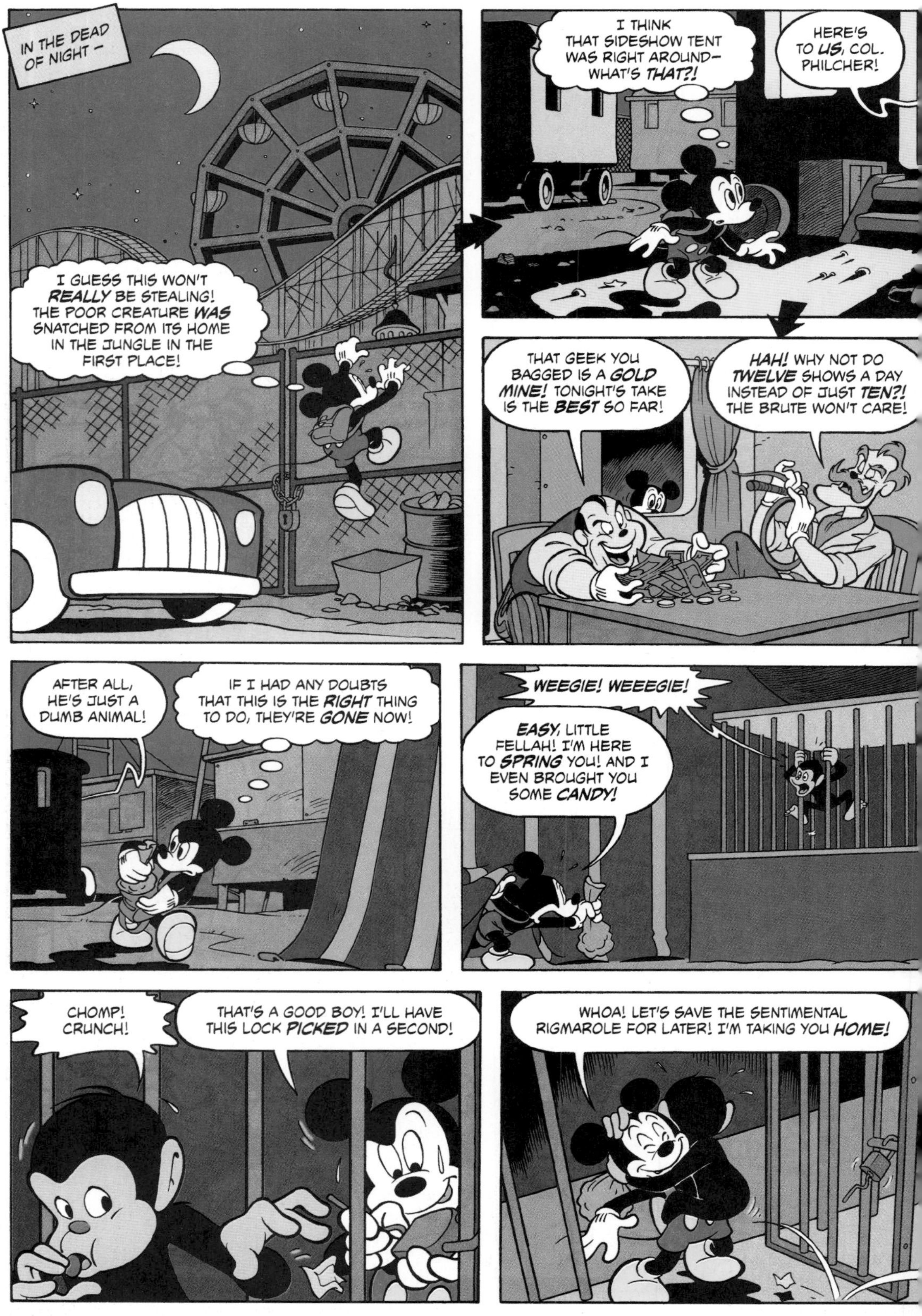
IN THE DEAD OF NIGHT –
I GUESS THIS WON'T REALLY BE STEALING! THE POOR CREATURE WAS SNATCHED FROM ITS HOME IN THE JUNGLE IN THE FIRST PLACE!
I THINK THAT SIDESHOW TENT WAS RIGHT AROUND– WHAT'S THAT?!
HERE'S TO US, COL. PHILCHER!
THAT GEEK YOU BAGGED IS A GOLD MINE! TONIGHT'S TAKE IS THE BEST SO FAR!
HAH! WHY NOT DO TWELVE SHOWS A DAY INSTEAD OF JUST TEN?! THE BRUTE WON'T CARE!
AFTER ALL, HE'S JUST A DUMB ANIMAL!
IF I HAD ANY DOUBTS THAT THIS IS THE RIGHT THING TO DO, THEY'RE GONE NOW!
WEEGIE! WEEEGIE!
EASY, LITTLE FELLAH! I'M HERE TO SPRING YOU! AND I EVEN BROUGHT YOU SOME CANDY!
CHOMP! CRUNCH!
THAT'S A GOOD BOY! I'LL HAVE THIS LOCK PICKED IN A SECOND!
WHOA! LET'S SAVE THE SENTIMENTAL RIGMAROLE FOR LATER! I'M TAKING YOU HOME!

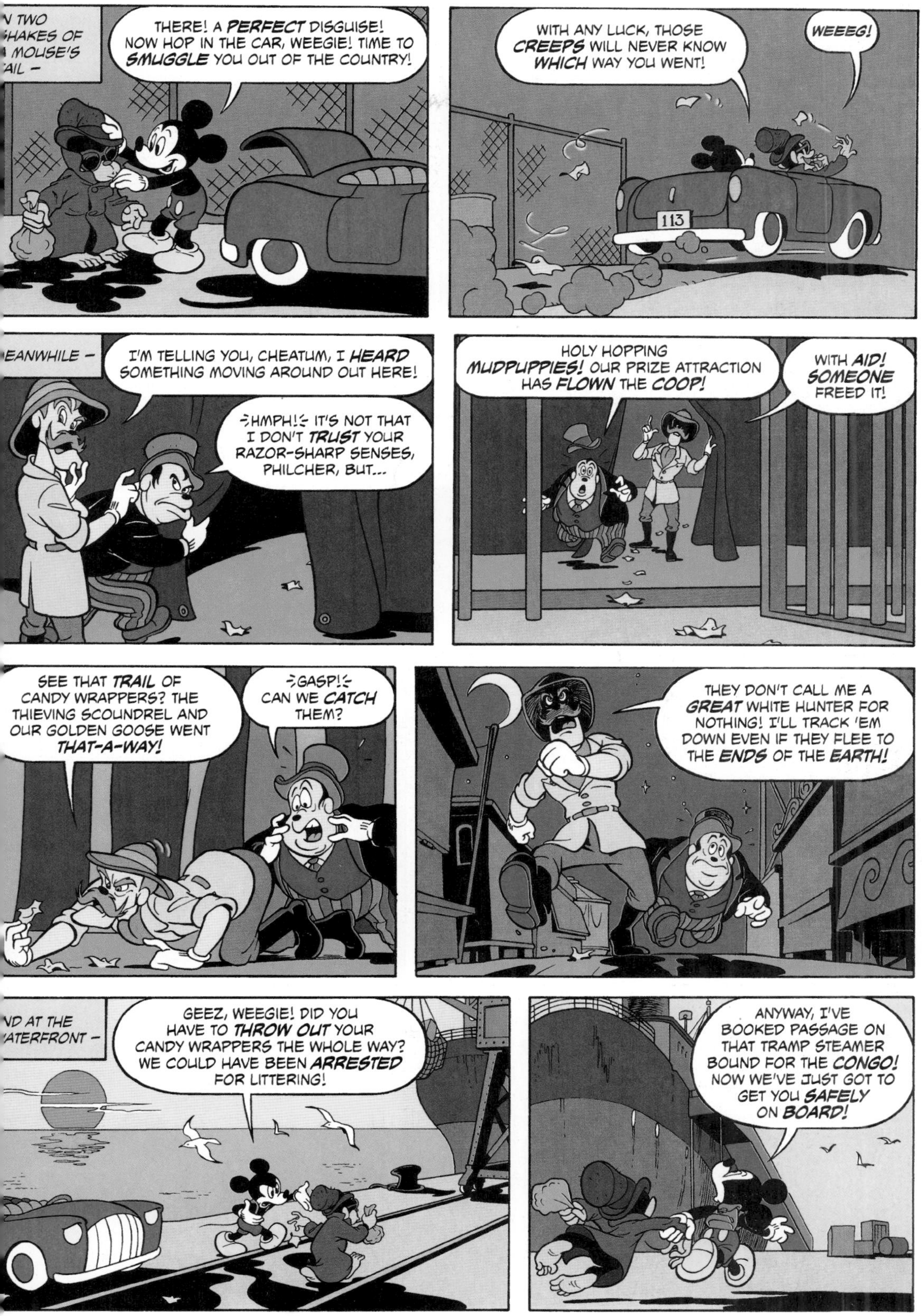
N TWO
SHAKES OF
A MOUSE'S
TAIL –
THERE! A PERFECT DISGUISE! NOW HOP IN THE CAR, WEEGIE! TIME TO SMUGGLE YOU OUT OF THE COUNTRY!
WITH ANY LUCK, THOSE CREEPS WILL NEVER KNOW WHICH WAY YOU WENT!
WEEEG!
113
EANWHILE –
I'M TELLING YOU, CHEATUM, I HEARD SOMETHING MOVING AROUND OUT HERE!
HMPH! IT'S NOT THAT I DON'T TRUST YOUR RAZOR-SHARP SENSES, PHILCHER, BUT...
HOLY HOPPING MUDPUPPIES! OUR PRIZE ATTRACTION HAS FLOWN THE COOP!
WITH AID! SOMEONE FREED IT!
SEE THAT TRAIL OF CANDY WRAPPERS? THE THIEVING SCOUNDREL AND OUR GOLDEN GOOSE WENT THAT-A-WAY!
GASP! CAN WE CATCH THEM?
THEY DON'T CALL ME A GREAT WHITE HUNTER FOR NOTHING! I'LL TRACK 'EM DOWN EVEN IF THEY FLEE TO THE ENDS OF THE EARTH!
ND AT THE
ATERFRONT –
GEEZ, WEEGIE! DID YOU HAVE TO THROW OUT YOUR CANDY WRAPPERS THE WHOLE WAY? WE COULD HAVE BEEN ARRESTED FOR LITTERING!
ANYWAY, I'VE BOOKED PASSAGE ON THAT TRAMP STEAMER BOUND FOR THE CONGO! NOW WE'VE JUST GOT TO GET YOU SAFELY ON BOARD!

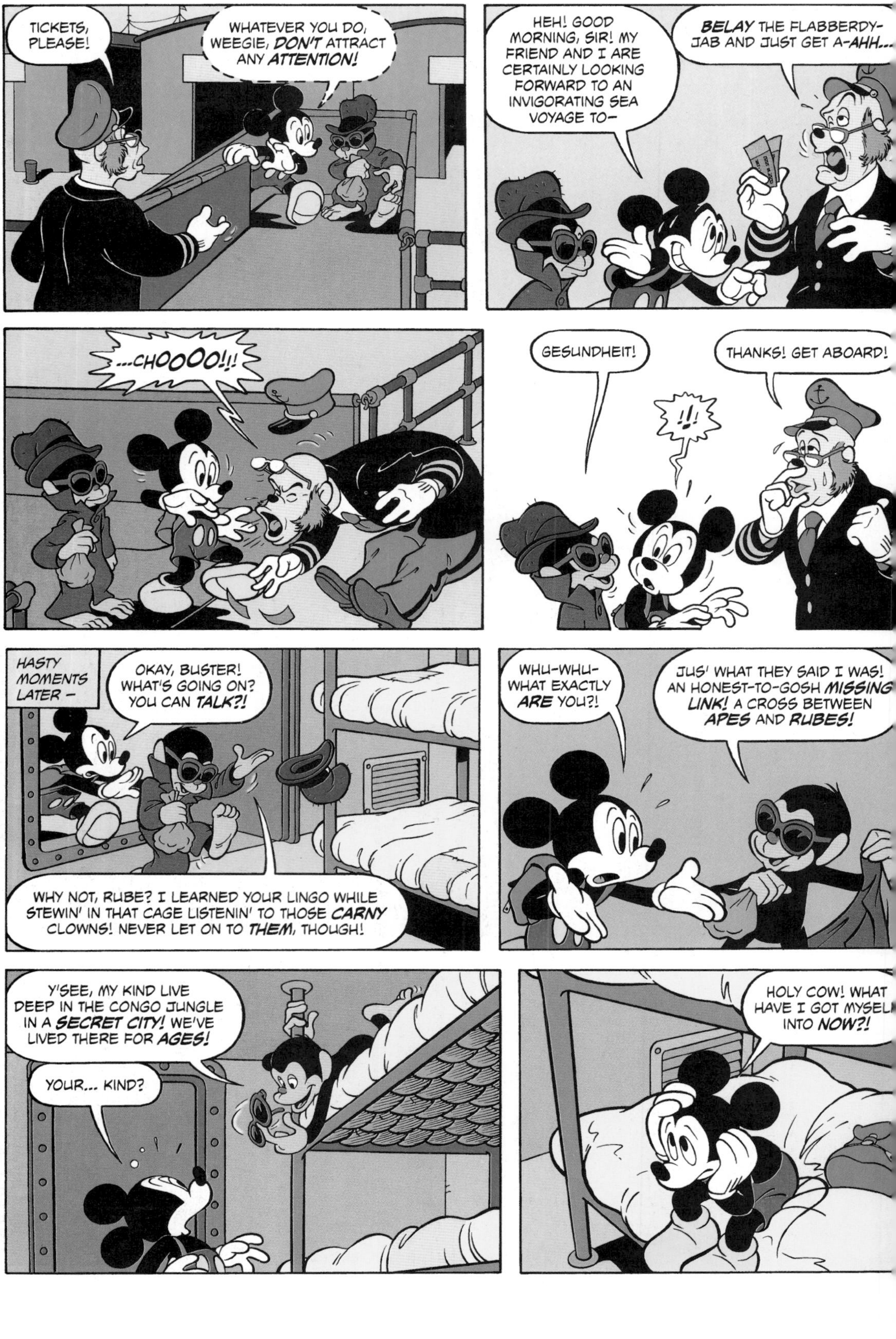

TICKETS, PLEASE!
WHATEVER YOU DO, WEEGIE, DON'T ATTRACT ANY ATTENTION!
HEH! GOOD MORNING, SIR! MY FRIEND AND I ARE CERTAINLY LOOKING FORWARD TO AN INVIGORATING SEA VOYAGE TO—
BELAY THE FLABBERDY-JAB AND JUST GET A-AHH...
...CHOOOO!!!
GESUNDHEIT!
THANKS! GET ABOARD!
!!
HASTY MOMENTS LATER —
OKAY, BUSTER! WHAT'S GOING ON? YOU CAN TALK?!
WHY NOT, RUBE? I LEARNED YOUR LINGO WHILE STEWIN' IN THAT CAGE LISTENIN' TO THOSE CARNY CLOWNS! NEVER LET ON TO THEM, THOUGH!
WHU-WHU-WHAT EXACTLY ARE YOU?!
JUS' WHAT THEY SAID I WAS! AN HONEST-TO-GOSH MISSING LINK! A CROSS BETWEEN APES AND RUBES!
Y'SEE, MY KIND LIVE DEEP IN THE CONGO JUNGLE IN A SECRET CITY! WE'VE LIVED THERE FOR AGES!
YOUR... KIND?
HOLY COW! WHAT HAVE I GOT MYSEL INTO NOW?!

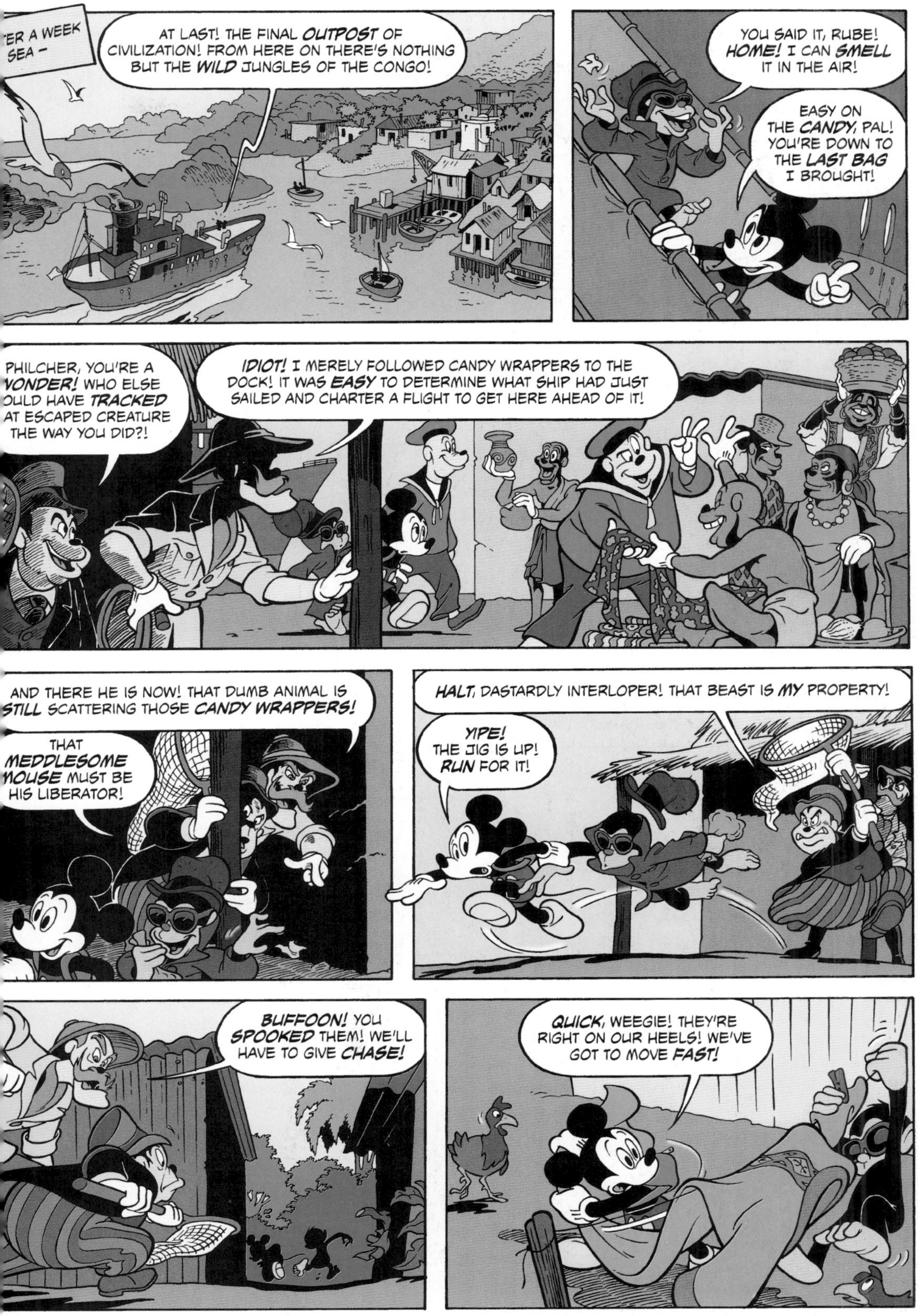

TER A WEEK
SEA –
AT LAST! THE FINAL OUTPOST OF CIVILIZATION! FROM HERE ON THERE'S NOTHING BUT THE WILD JUNGLES OF THE CONGO!
YOU SAID IT, RUBE! HOME! I CAN SMELL IT IN THE AIR!
EASY ON THE CANDY, PAL! YOU'RE DOWN TO THE LAST BAG I BROUGHT!
PHILCHER, YOU'RE A WONDER! WHO ELSE OULD HAVE TRACKED AT ESCAPED CREATURE THE WAY YOU DID?!
IDIOT! I MERELY FOLLOWED CANDY WRAPPERS TO THE DOCK! IT WAS EASY TO DETERMINE WHAT SHIP HAD JUST SAILED AND CHARTER A FLIGHT TO GET HERE AHEAD OF IT!
AND THERE HE IS NOW! THAT DUMB ANIMAL IS STILL SCATTERING THOSE CANDY WRAPPERS!
THAT MEDDLESOME MOUSE MUST BE HIS LIBERATOR!
HALT, DASTARDLY INTERLOPER! THAT BEAST IS MY PROPERTY!
YIPE! THE JIG IS UP! RUN FOR IT!
BUFFOON! YOU SPOOKED THEM! WE'LL HAVE TO GIVE CHASE!
QUICK, WEEGIE! THEY'RE RIGHT ON OUR HEELS! WE'VE GOT TO MOVE FAST!

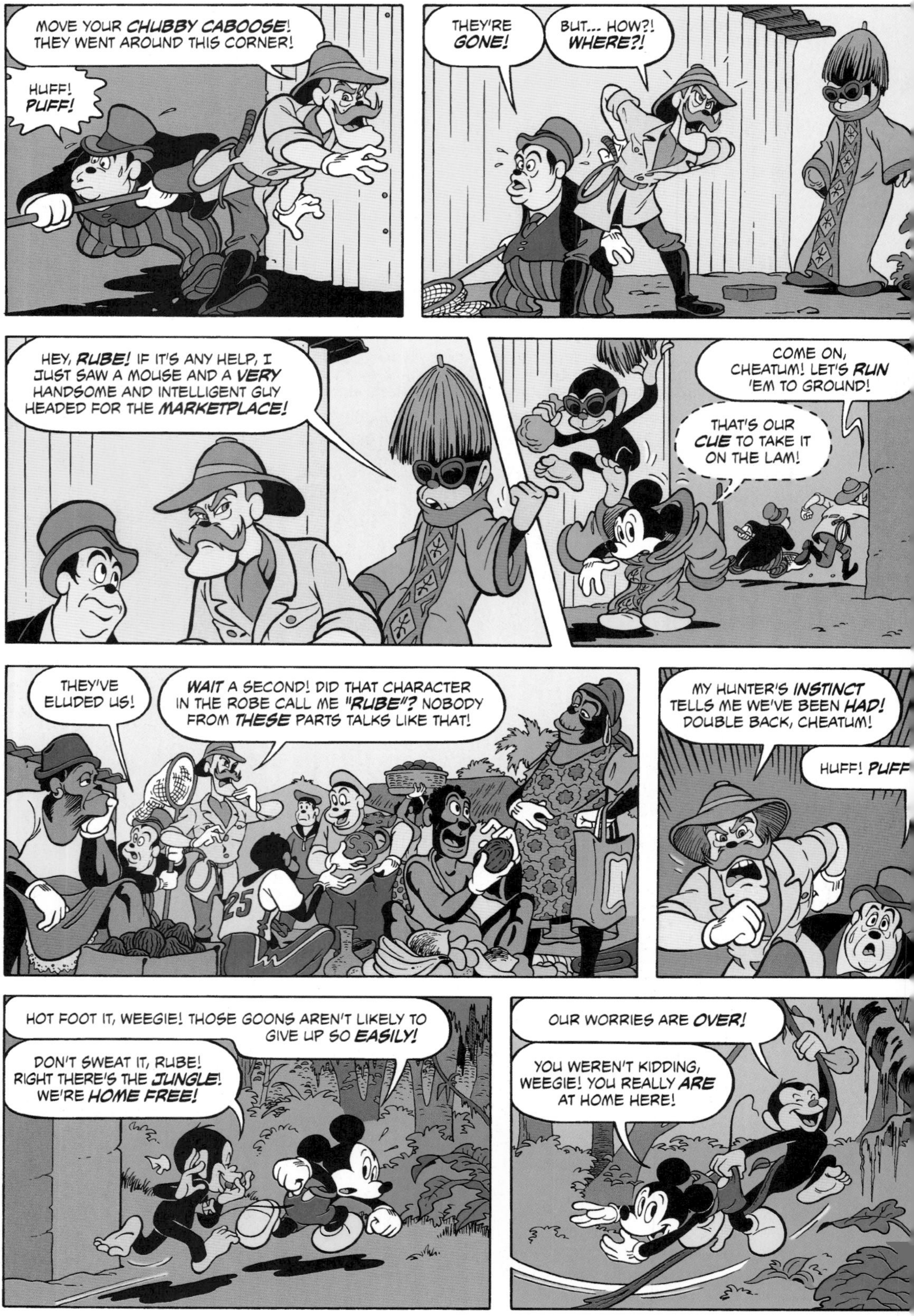

MOVE YOUR CHUBBY CABOOSE! THEY WENT AROUND THIS CORNER!
HUFF! PUFF!
THEY'RE GONE!
BUT... HOW?! WHERE?!
HEY, RUBE! IF IT'S ANY HELP, I JUST SAW A MOUSE AND A VERY HANDSOME AND INTELLIGENT GUY HEADED FOR THE MARKETPLACE!
COME ON, CHEATUM! LET'S RUN 'EM TO GROUND!
THAT'S OUR CUE TO TAKE IT ON THE LAM!
THEY'VE ELUDED US!
WAIT A SECOND! DID THAT CHARACTER IN THE ROBE CALL ME "RUBE"? NOBODY FROM THESE PARTS TALKS LIKE THAT!
MY HUNTER'S INSTINCT TELLS ME WE'VE BEEN HAD! DOUBLE BACK, CHEATUM!
HUFF! PUFF
HOT FOOT IT, WEEGIE! THOSE GOONS AREN'T LIKELY TO GIVE UP SO EASILY!
DON'T SWEAT IT, RUBE! RIGHT THERE'S THE JUNGLE! WE'RE HOME FREE!
OUR WORRIES ARE OVER!
YOU WEREN'T KIDDING, WEEGIE! YOU REALLY ARE AT HOME HERE!

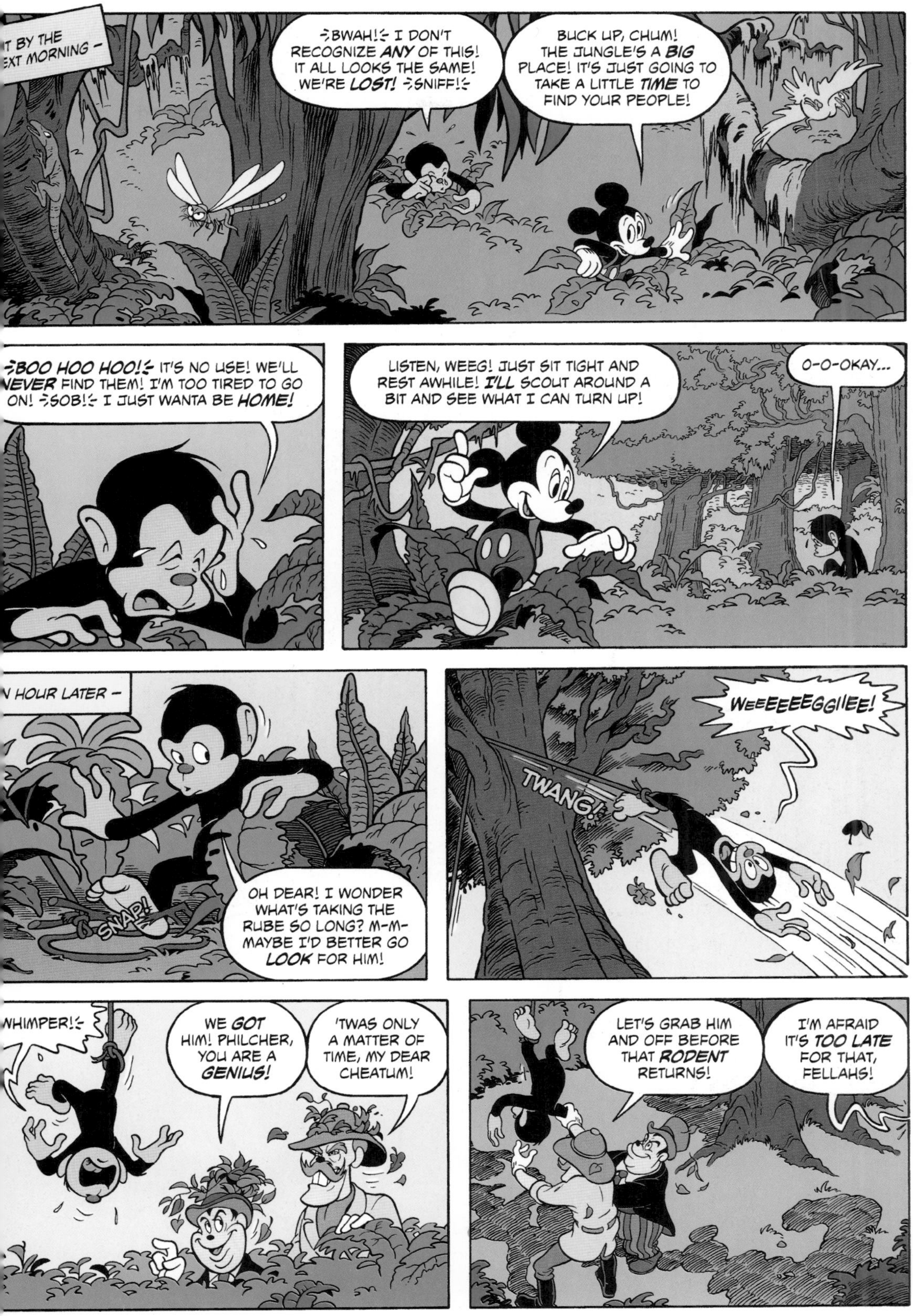
T BY THE
EXT MORNING –
-BWAH!- I DON'T RECOGNIZE ANY OF THIS! IT ALL LOOKS THE SAME! WE'RE LOST! -SNIFF!-
BUCK UP, CHUM! THE JUNGLE'S A BIG PLACE! IT'S JUST GOING TO TAKE A LITTLE TIME TO FIND YOUR PEOPLE!
-BOO HOO HOO!- IT'S NO USE! WE'LL NEVER FIND THEM! I'M TOO TIRED TO GO ON! -SOB!- I JUST WANTA BE HOME!
LISTEN, WEEG! JUST SIT TIGHT AND REST AWHILE! I'LL SCOUT AROUND A BIT AND SEE WHAT I CAN TURN UP!
O-O-OKAY...
N HOUR LATER –
OH DEAR! I WONDER WHAT'S TAKING THE RUBE SO LONG? M-M-MAYBE I'D BETTER GO LOOK FOR HIM!
SNAP!
WEEEEEEGGIIEE!
TWANG!
WHIMPER!-
WE GOT HIM! PHILCHER, YOU ARE A GENIUS!
'TWAS ONLY A MATTER OF TIME, MY DEAR CHEATUM!
LET'S GRAB HIM AND OFF BEFORE THAT RODENT RETURNS!
I'M AFRAID IT'S TOO LATE FOR THAT, FELLAHS!

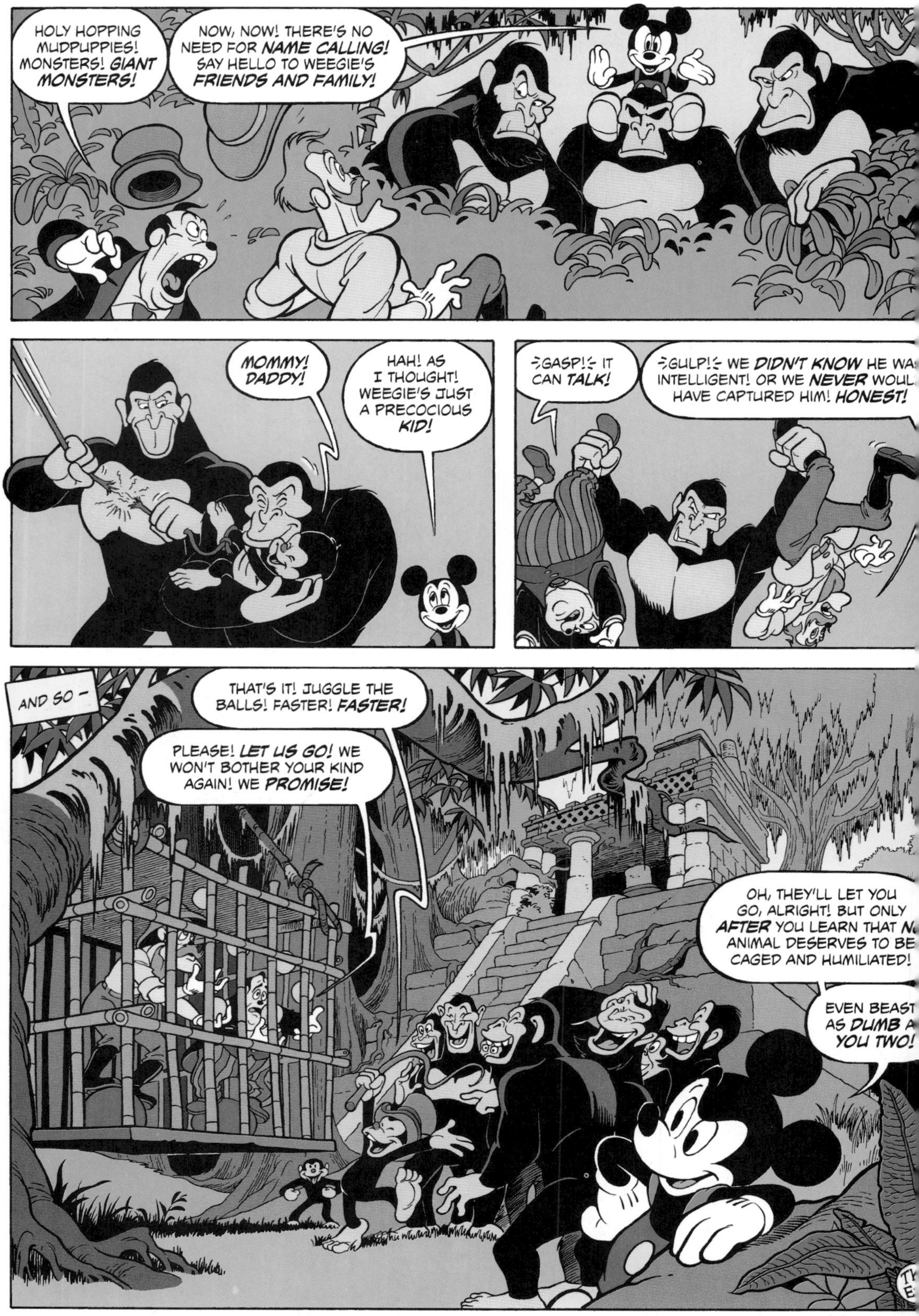
HOLY HOPPING MUDPUPPIES! MONSTERS! GIANT MONSTERS!
NOW, NOW! THERE'S NO NEED FOR NAME CALLING! SAY HELLO TO WEEGIE'S FRIENDS AND FAMILY!
MOMMY! DADDY!
HAH! AS I THOUGHT! WEEGIE'S JUST A PRECOCIOUS KID!
-GASP!- IT CAN TALK!
-GULP!- WE DIDN'T KNOW HE WA
INTELLIGENT! OR WE NEVER WOUL
HAVE CAPTURED HIM! HONEST!
AND SO –
THAT'S IT! JUGGLE THE BALLS! FASTER! FASTER!
PLEASE! LET US GO! WE WON'T BOTHER YOUR KIND AGAIN! WE PROMISE!
OH, THEY'LL LET YOU GO, ALRIGHT! BUT ONLY AFTER YOU LEARN THAT N
ANIMAL DESERVES TO BE CAGED AND HUMILIATED!
EVEN BEAST AS DUMB A YOU TWO!

Gemstone Publishing presents

More Life and Times of $CROOGE McDUCK

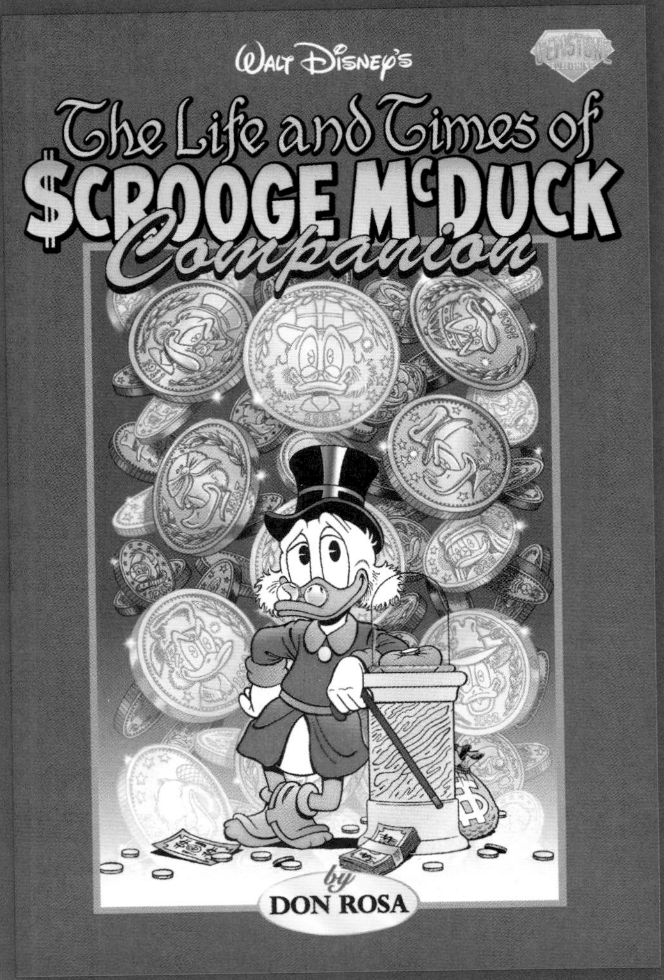

Walt Disney's
The Life and Times of
$CROOGE McDUCK
Companion
by
DON ROSA

You asked for them, and here they are... the prequels, the sequels, and the in-betweenquels to Don Rosa's *Life and Times of Scrooge McDuck!* Filling in the gaps between the twelve original chapters are "The Cowboy Captain of the Cutty Sark" (Chapter 3B/*Uncle Scrooge* 318), "The Vigilante of Pizen Bluff" (Chapter 6B/*US* 306), "The Prisoner of White Agony Creek" (the all-new Chapter 8B!), "Hearts of the Yukon" (Chapter 8C/*Walt Disney Giant* 1) and "The Sharpie of the Culebra Cut" (Chapter 10B/*US* 332).

But wait... there's more! We've got Don's first look at Scrooge's youth—the famous flashback from "Last Sled to Dawson" (*Uncle Scrooge Adventures* 5). We've got the apocrypha: "Of Ducks and Dimes and Destinies" (Chapter 0/*US* 297) and "The Dream of a Lifetime!" (*US* 329), with the modern-day Magica De Spell and Beagle Boys wreaking havoc in Scrooge's past. And we've got the commentary—more than a dozen pages of Rosa recollections on how these classics came to be, all for only $16.99!

STILL ON SALE (NOW IN ITS SECOND PRINTING!)

It's Rosa's original twelve-chapter quest into Scrooge's life—presented in a 264-page volume replete with extensive authorial commentary. From Scrooge's Scottish childhood to his worldwide quest for gold; from his ill-starred romances to his meetings with history's heroes, this classic biography marked a milestone in duck comics. Annotated by Rosa himself and full of new-to-North-America art. So popular it's now in its second printing, Gemstone's $17.99 collected edition belongs on every Disney fan's bookshelf.

GEMSTONE PUBLISHING

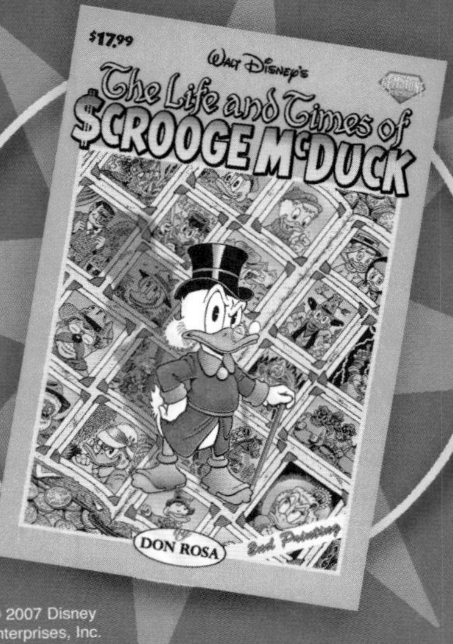

$17.99
Walt Disney's
The Life and Times of
$CROOGE McDUCK
DON ROSA

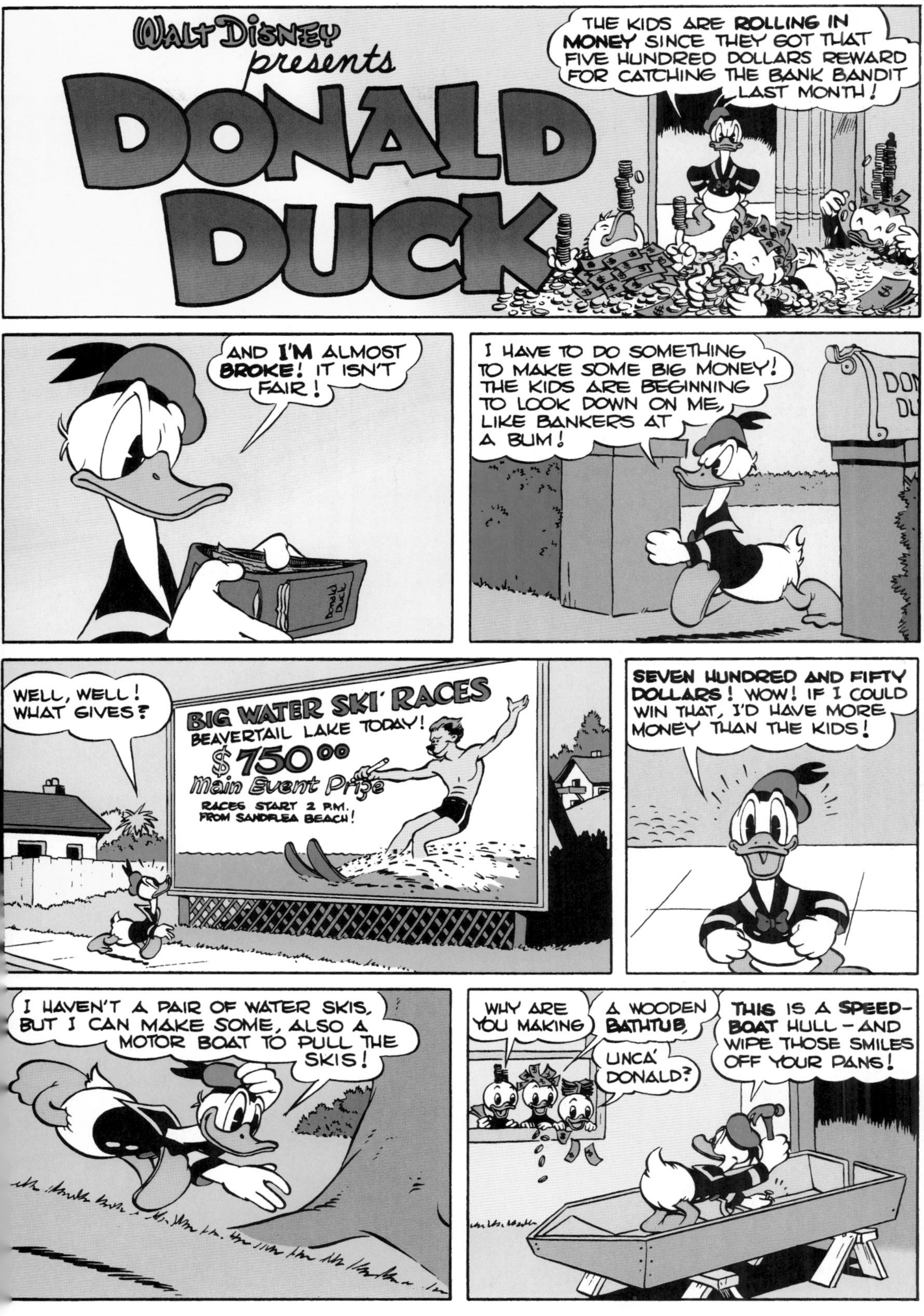
WALT DISNEY presents
DONALD DUCK
THE KIDS ARE ROLLING IN MONEY SINCE THEY GOT THAT FIVE HUNDRED DOLLARS REWARD FOR CATCHING THE BANK BANDIT LAST MONTH!
AND I'M ALMOST BROKE! IT ISN'T FAIR!
Donald Duck
I HAVE TO DO SOMETHING TO MAKE SOME BIG MONEY! THE KIDS ARE BEGINNING TO LOOK DOWN ON ME, LIKE BANKERS AT A BUM!
WELL, WELL! WHAT GIVES?
BIG WATER SKI' RACES
BEAVERTAIL LAKE TODAY!
$750.00
Main Event Prize
RACES START 2 P.M. FROM SANDFLEA BEACH!
SEVEN HUNDRED AND FIFTY DOLLARS! WOW! IF I COULD WIN THAT, I'D HAVE MORE MONEY THAN THE KIDS!
I HAVEN'T A PAIR OF WATER SKIS, BUT I CAN MAKE SOME, ALSO A MOTOR BOAT TO PULL THE SKIS!
WHY ARE YOU MAKING
A WOODEN BATHTUB,
UNCA' DONALD?
THIS IS A SPEED-BOAT HULL - AND WIPE THOSE SMILES OFF YOUR PANS!

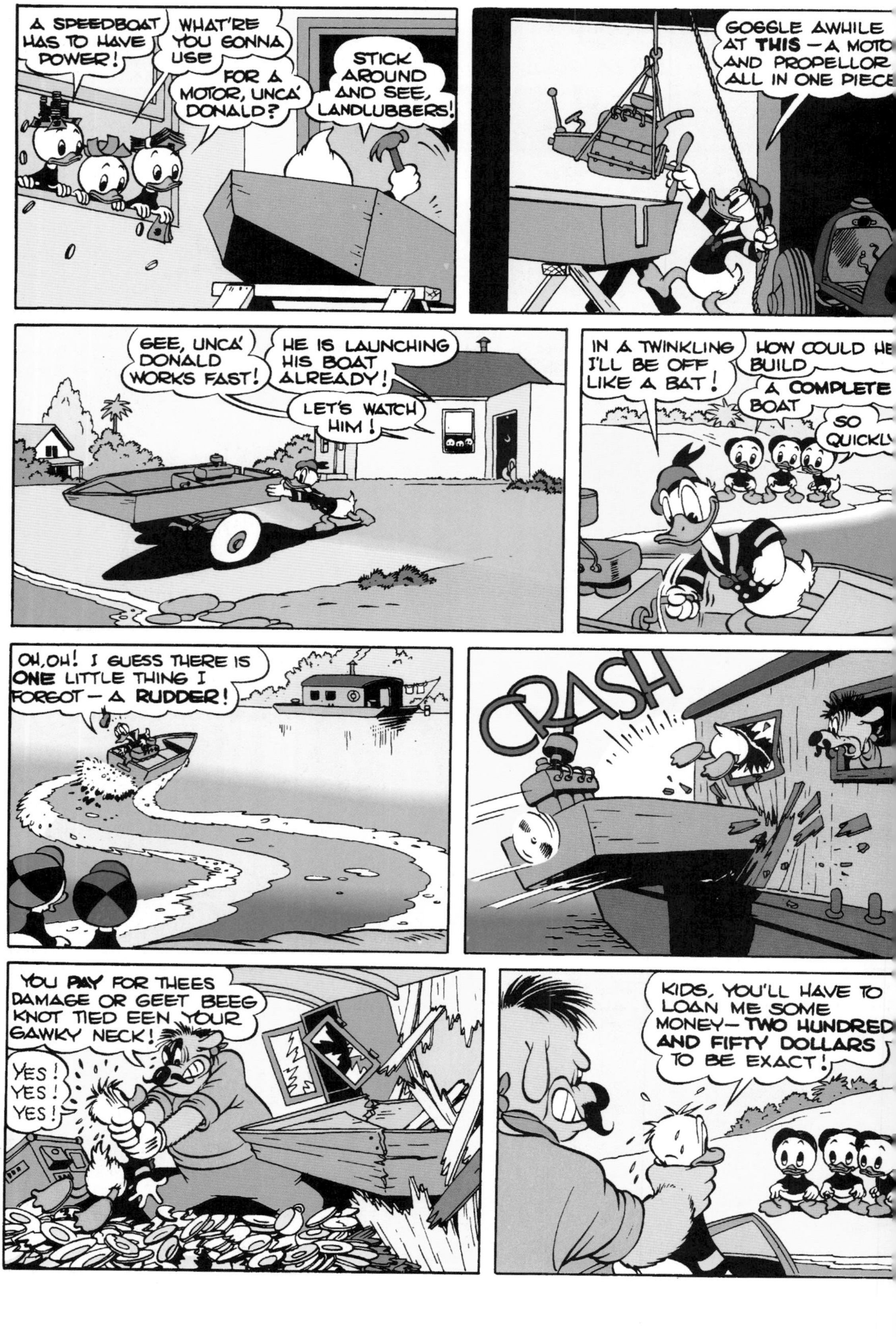
A SPEEDBOAT HAS TO HAVE POWER!
WHAT'RE YOU GONNA USE FOR A MOTOR, UNCA' DONALD?
STICK AROUND AND SEE, LANDLUBBERS!
GOGGLE AWHILE AT THIS — A MOTO AND PROPELLOR ALL IN ONE PIECE
GEE, UNCA' DONALD WORKS FAST!
HE IS LAUNCHING HIS BOAT ALREADY!
LET'S WATCH HIM!
IN A TWINKLING I'LL BE OFF LIKE A BAT!
HOW COULD HE BUILD A COMPLETE BOAT SO QUICKLY
OH, OH! I GUESS THERE IS ONE LITTLE THING I FORGOT — A RUDDER!
CRASH
YOU PAY FOR THEES DAMAGE OR GEET BEEG KNOT TIED EEN YOUR GAWKY NECK!
YES! YES! YES!
KIDS, YOU'LL HAVE TO LOAN ME SOME MONEY— TWO HUNDRED AND FIFTY DOLLARS TO BE EXACT!

OH, WELL, AFTER PAYING BACK THE TWO-FIFTY OUT OF THE PRIZE MONEY, I'LL STILL HAVE FIVE HUNDRED, WHICH'LL MAKE ME JUST AS RICH AS THE KIDS!

WHO IS GOING TO **DRIVE** YOUR BOAT WHILE YOU RIDE THE WATER SKIS, UNCA' DONALD?

YOU KIDS WILL DRIVE IT!

AND I **KNOW** YOU'LL DO A GOOD JOB, FOR IF I **DON'T** WIN THE RACE, YOU WON'T SEE YOUR TWO HUNDRED AND FIFTY BUCKS AGAIN!

GET IN, KIDS, AND TAKE THE CONTROLS! I WANT TO TRY OUT MY WATER SKIS!

A LITTLE MORE SPEED, BOYS – BUT NOT TOO MUCH!

WOW! THIS IS DANGEROUS SPORT! LOOK AT THAT GIRL WATCH! SHE THINKS I'M HOT STUFF!

SHE'S CLAPPING HER HANDS! I DIDN'T THINK I WAS **QUITE** THAT GOOD!

OH, POPS, YOU'RE WONDERFUL!

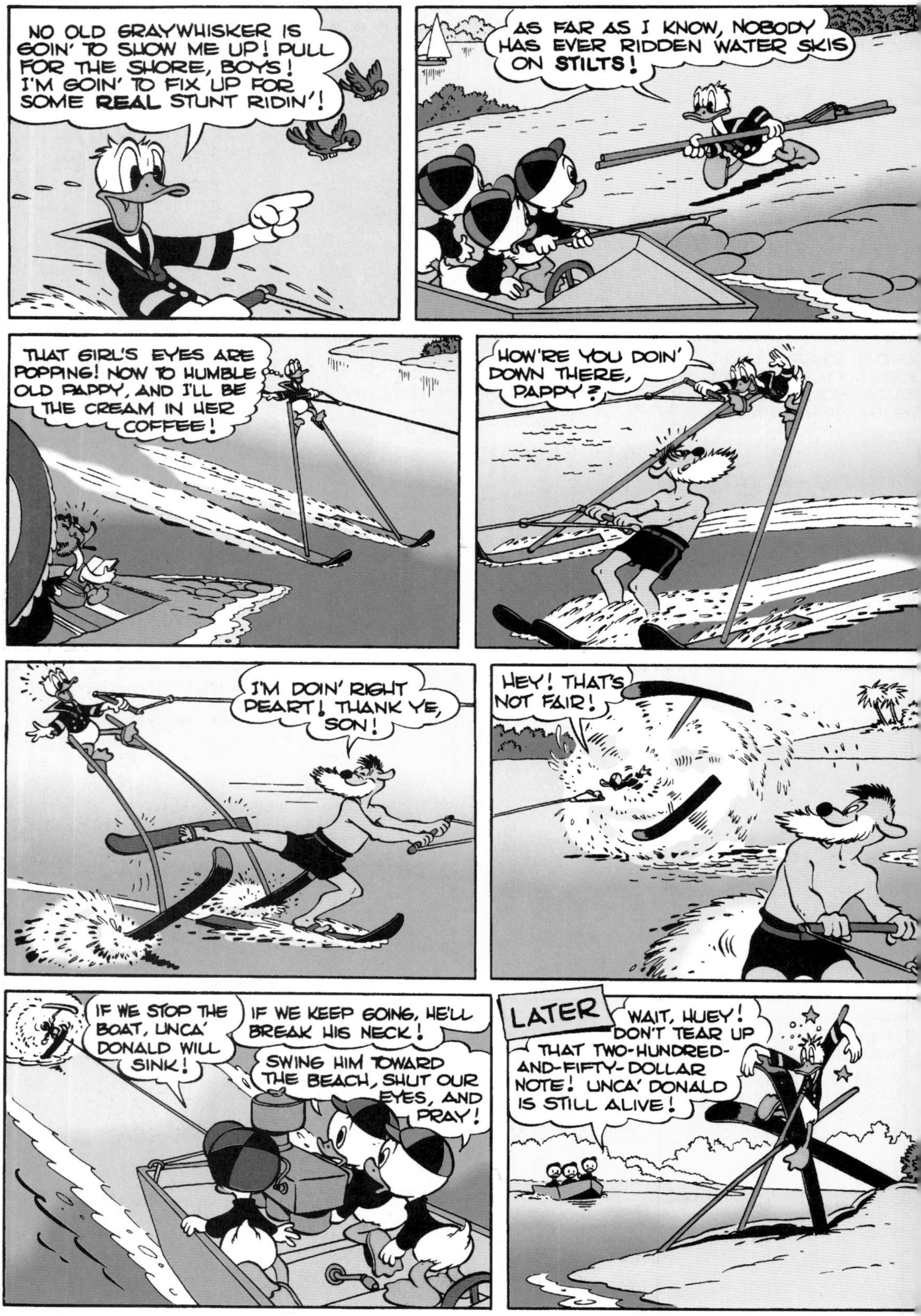
NO OLD GRAYWHISKER IS GOIN' TO SHOW ME UP! PULL FOR THE SHORE, BOYS! I'M GOIN' TO FIX UP FOR SOME REAL STUNT RIDIN'!
AS FAR AS I KNOW, NOBODY HAS EVER RIDDEN WATER SKIS ON STILTS!
THAT GIRL'S EYES ARE POPPING! NOW TO HUMBLE OLD PAPPY, AND I'LL BE THE CREAM IN HER COFFEE!
HOW'RE YOU DOIN' DOWN THERE, PAPPY?
I'M DOIN' RIGHT PEART! THANK YE, SON!
HEY! THAT'S NOT FAIR!
IF WE STOP THE BOAT, UNCA' DONALD WILL SINK!
IF WE KEEP GOING, HE'LL BREAK HIS NECK!
SWING HIM TOWARD THE BEACH, SHUT OUR EYES, AND PRAY!
LATER
WAIT, HUEY! DON'T TEAR UP THAT TWO-HUNDRED-AND-FIFTY-DOLLAR NOTE! UNCA' DONALD IS STILL ALIVE!

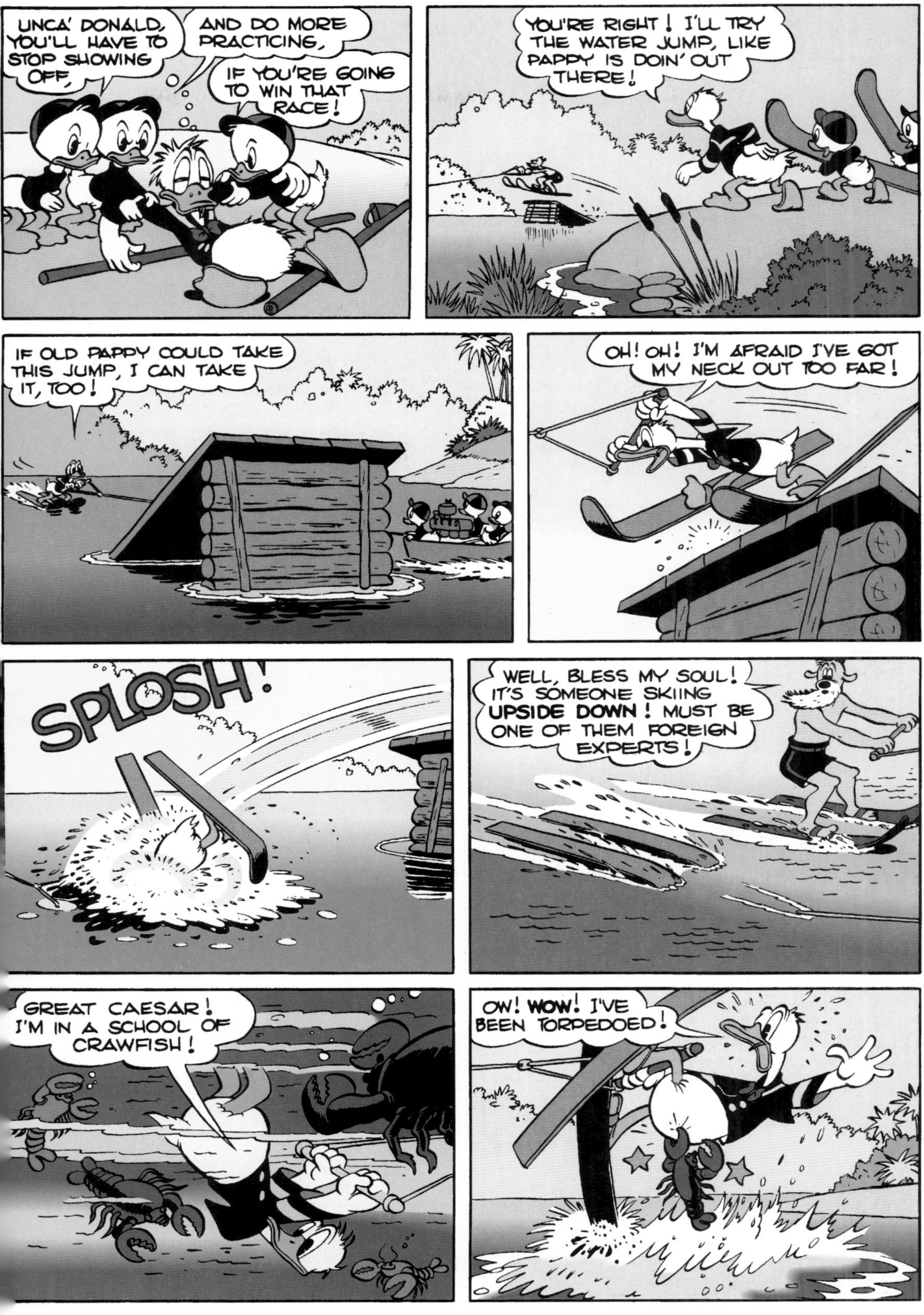
UNCA' DONALD, YOU'LL HAVE TO STOP SHOWING OFF,
AND DO MORE PRACTICING,
IF YOU'RE GOING TO WIN THAT RACE!
YOU'RE RIGHT! I'LL TRY THE WATER JUMP, LIKE PAPPY IS DOIN' OUT THERE!
IF OLD PAPPY COULD TAKE THIS JUMP, I CAN TAKE IT, TOO!
OH! OH! I'M AFRAID I'VE GOT MY NECK OUT TOO FAR!
SPLOSH!
WELL, BLESS MY SOUL! IT'S SOMEONE SKIING **UPSIDE DOWN**! MUST BE ONE OF THEM FOREIGN EXPERTS!
GREAT CAESAR! I'M IN A SCHOOL OF CRAWFISH!
OW! **WOW**! I'VE BEEN TORPEDOED!

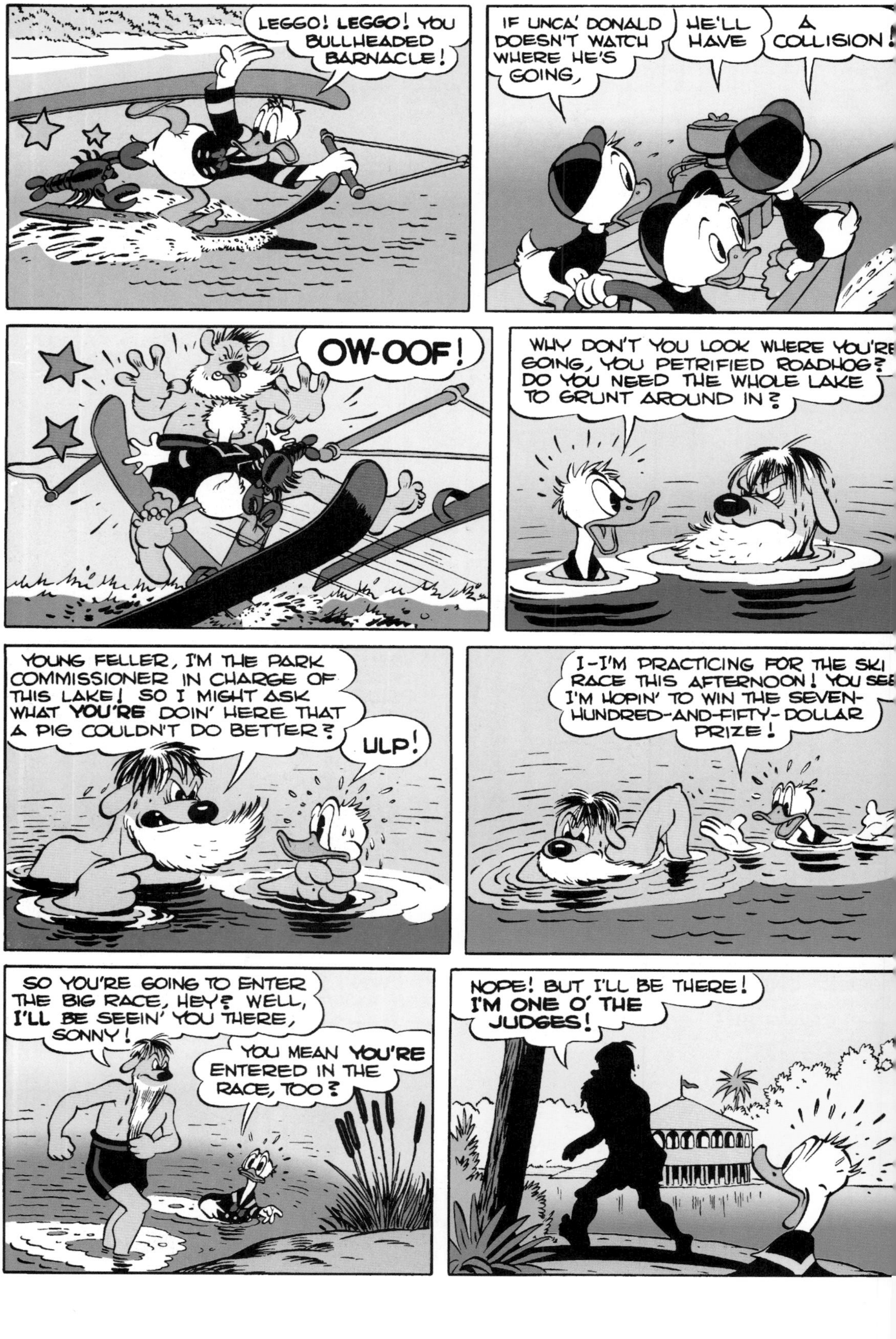
LEGGO! LEGGO! YOU BULLHEADED BARNACLE!
IF UNCA' DONALD DOESN'T WATCH WHERE HE'S GOING,
HE'LL HAVE
A COLLISION!
OW-OOF!
WHY DON'T YOU LOOK WHERE YOU'RE GOING, YOU PETRIFIED ROADHOG? DO YOU NEED THE WHOLE LAKE TO GRUNT AROUND IN?
YOUNG FELLER, I'M THE PARK COMMISSIONER IN CHARGE OF THIS LAKE! SO I MIGHT ASK WHAT YOU'RE DOIN' HERE THAT A PIG COULDN'T DO BETTER?
ULP!
I-I'M PRACTICING FOR THE SKI RACE THIS AFTERNOON! YOU SEE I'M HOPIN' TO WIN THE SEVEN-HUNDRED-AND-FIFTY-DOLLAR PRIZE!
SO YOU'RE GOING TO ENTER THE BIG RACE, HEY? WELL, I'LL BE SEEIN' YOU THERE, SONNY!
YOU MEAN YOU'RE ENTERED IN THE RACE, TOO?
NOPE! BUT I'LL BE THERE! I'M ONE O' THE JUDGES!

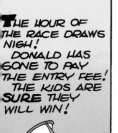

THE HOUR OF THE RACE DRAWS NIGH! DONALD HAS GONE TO PAY THE ENTRY FEE! THE KIDS ARE *SURE* THEY WILL WIN!

I FEEL LIKE CELEBRATING!

SO DO I!

A LITTLE SODA POP AND STUFF WILL PUT US RIGHT ON EDGE!

I THINK WE SHOULD GET SOME HOT DOGS, TOO!

AND SOME STICK CANDY!

AND SOME BUTTERSCOTCH ICE CREAM!

WE'LL YANK UNCA' DONALD ACROSS THE FINISH LINE A BLOCK AHEAD OF EVERYBODY!

TWO BLOCKS!

TWO MILES!

WE'LL SET A NEW *WORLD'S* RECORD!

NOW YOU'RE TALKIN'!

STOP HOARDING THAT CASHEW NUT FUDGE!

PAY FEES HERE

YOUR NAME, PLEASE!

DONALD DUCK!

WHO WILL DRIVE YOUR BOAT, MR. DUCK?

MY NEPHEWS, HUEY, LOUIE, AND DEWEY!

HERE IS YOUR ENTRY CARD! ANY CHANGES OF DRIVERS OR EQUIPMENT WILL DISQUALIFY YOU FROM THE RACE!

YESSIR!

I HOPE THE KIDS HAVE THE BOAT GASSED UP AND READY TO ROAR!

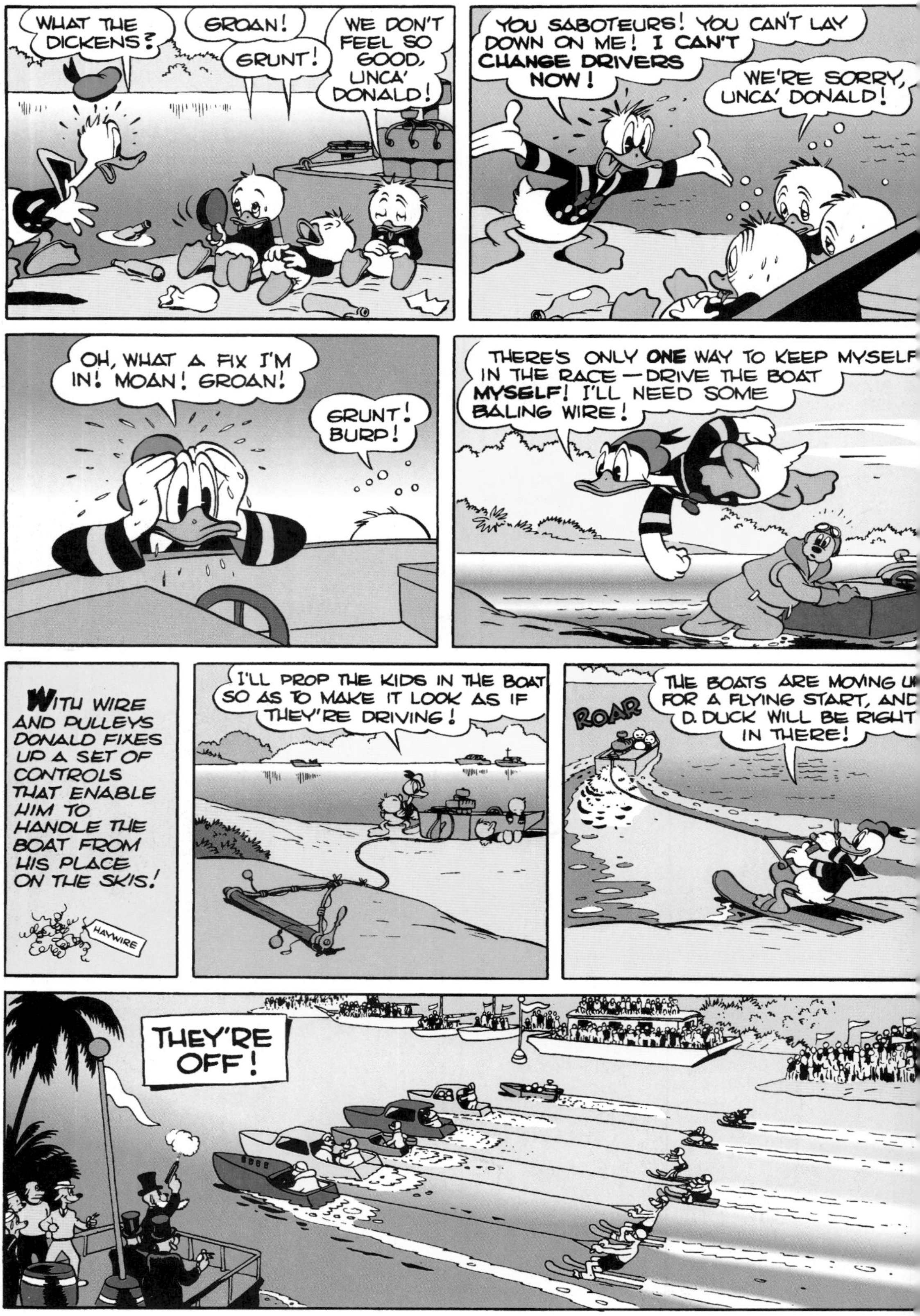
WHAT THE DICKENS?
GROAN!
GRUNT!
WE DON'T FEEL SO GOOD, UNCA' DONALD!
YOU SABOTEURS! YOU CAN'T LAY DOWN ON ME! I CAN'T CHANGE DRIVERS NOW!
WE'RE SORRY, UNCA' DONALD!
OH, WHAT A FIX I'M IN! MOAN! GROAN!
GRUNT! BURP!
THERE'S ONLY ONE WAY TO KEEP MYSELF IN THE RACE — DRIVE THE BOAT MYSELF! I'LL NEED SOME BALING WIRE!
WITH WIRE AND PULLEYS DONALD FIXES UP A SET OF CONTROLS THAT ENABLE HIM TO HANDLE THE BOAT FROM HIS PLACE ON THE SKIS!
HAYWIRE
I'LL PROP THE KIDS IN THE BOAT SO AS TO MAKE IT LOOK AS IF THEY'RE DRIVING!
ROAR
THE BOATS ARE MOVING UP FOR A FLYING START, AND D. DUCK WILL BE RIGHT IN THERE!
THEY'RE OFF!

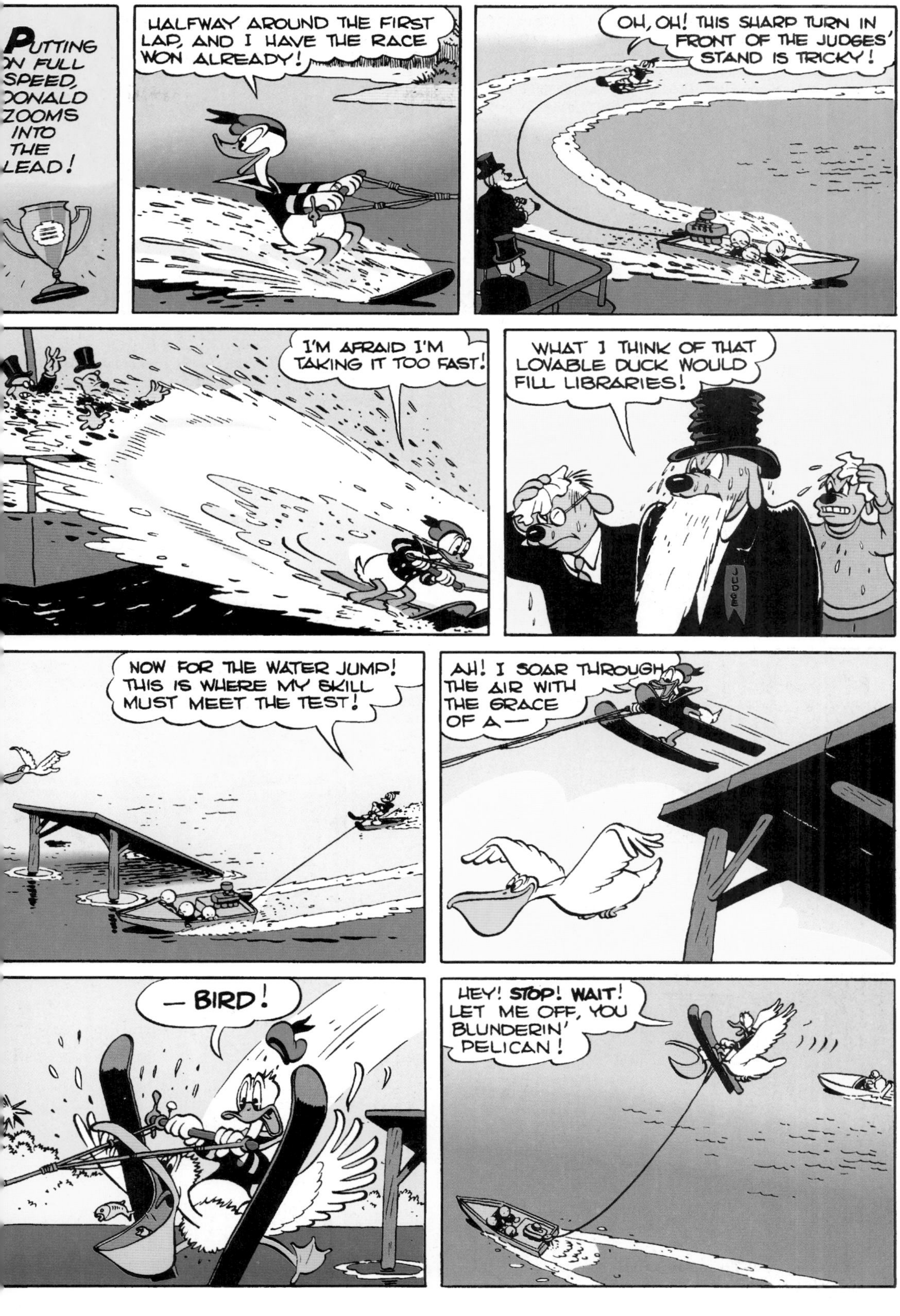

PUTTING ON FULL SPEED, DONALD ZOOMS INTO THE LEAD!
HALFWAY AROUND THE FIRST LAP, AND I HAVE THE RACE WON ALREADY!
OH, OH! THIS SHARP TURN IN FRONT OF THE JUDGES' STAND IS TRICKY!
I'M AFRAID I'M TAKING IT TOO FAST!
WHAT I THINK OF THAT LOVABLE DUCK WOULD FILL LIBRARIES!
JUDGE
NOW FOR THE WATER JUMP! THIS IS WHERE MY SKILL MUST MEET THE TEST!
AH! I SOAR THROUGH THE AIR WITH THE GRACE OF A—
—BIRD!
HEY! STOP! WAIT! LET ME OFF, YOU BLUNDERIN' PELICAN!

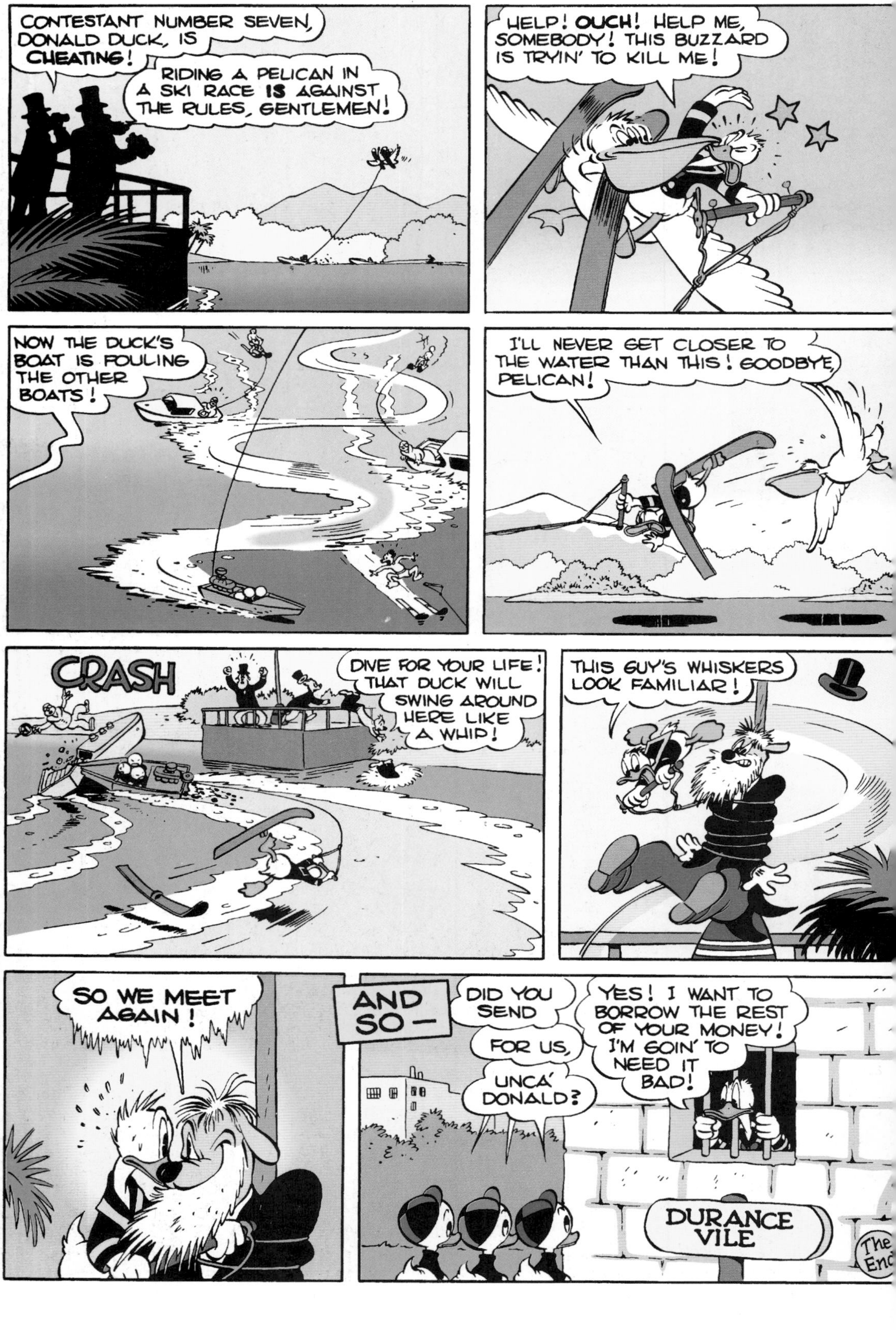
CONTESTANT NUMBER SEVEN, DONALD DUCK, IS CHEATING!
RIDING A PELICAN IN A SKI RACE IS AGAINST THE RULES, GENTLEMEN!
HELP! OUCH! HELP ME, SOMEBODY! THIS BUZZARD IS TRYIN' TO KILL ME!
NOW THE DUCK'S BOAT IS FOULING THE OTHER BOATS!
I'LL NEVER GET CLOSER TO THE WATER THAN THIS! GOODBYE, PELICAN!
CRASH
DIVE FOR YOUR LIFE! THAT DUCK WILL SWING AROUND HERE LIKE A WHIP!
THIS GUY'S WHISKERS LOOK FAMILIAR!
SO WE MEET AGAIN!
AND SO —
DID YOU SEND
FOR US,
UNCA' DONALD?
YES! I WANT TO BORROW THE REST OF YOUR MONEY! I'M GOIN' TO NEED IT BAD!
DURANCE VILE
The End